Praise for *Us*

"Michael Kimball never ceases to astonish. He is a hero of contemporary fiction."

— Sam Lipsyte

"A deep love between an ageing husband and wife is given a heartbreaking voice ... tender and poignant"

— *Time Out London*

"Be warned: this book has the power to make even the most hard-hearted of readers shed a tear. ... Kimball has broken into new territory: *Us* is one of the most graphic depictions of illness and loss I have ever read."

— *The Glasgow Herald*

"Haunting and awesome ... beautiful and intense ... This is a novel from a great talent."

— *El País* (Spain)

"Powerful and moving ... breathless"

— *Observer*

"A monument to love"

— *El Placer de la Lectura* (Spain)

"Bathed in tenderness ... touching and breathtaking ... one of the most moving, heartbreaking, and sad novels of contemporary American fiction. It is essential."

— *El Razón* (México)

"This is the saddest book I have ever read and one of the most beautiful and unusual. ... One can't help being aware of his grief and the great love he feels for his dying wife. It will make you cry and break your heart but this is one book you must read."

— *Telegraph and Argus*

"First, Camus showed us the human condition. Now Kimball has ... with a fluid style and a dizzying empathy. Kimball is a great writer."

— *El Mercurio* (Chile)

"Kimball has created something rare and brave ... [It is a] beautifully tuned, near perfect account of a very ordinary death."

— *Metro London*

"There are two books I can remember that ever made me physically cry. There were the rape scenes in Saramago's *Blindness*, and there was nearly every chapter of Michael Kimball's *[Us]*. While the first hurt because it was so brutal, Kimball's was a softer kind of invocation—as I read it in a bathtub, I could not shake the feeling of being held, as if somehow the words had interlaced my skin. This is the essence of the magic Michael Kimball holds—his sentences come on so taut, so right there, and yet somehow so calming, it's as if you are being visited by some lighted presence."

— Blake Butler

Praise for Michael Kimball's Other Novels

"Occasionally a novel by a new writer will cause critics to choke with excitement. This is one. ... Kimball resembles a skinhead at a cocktail party—no quarter given to poxy commercialism. For that reason alone, his achievement is admirable."

— *The Scotsman*

"[Michael Kimball] has taken it [American literature] somewhere very dark and unsettling."

— *The Times*

Michael Kimball "has already delivered the future of the novel ... [He is] one of the authentic innovators in contemporary fiction."

— *Letras Libres* (Mexico)

"Kimball creates a sort of curatorial masterpiece, finding the perfect spot for everything that a life comprises."

— *The Believer*

"There is a whole life contained in this slim novel, a life as funny and warm and sad and heartbreaking as any other, rendered with honest complexity and freshness by Kimball's sharp writing."

— *Los Angeles Times*

"I don't always say this, so I hope you will indulge me: Read *Dear Everybody*. It is a work of literary inventiveness and great compassion."

— WETA's *The Book Studio*

[*Dear Everybody* is] "one of the hottest, most innovative books of the year"

— *Htmlgiant*

"*Dear Everybody* has the page-turning urgency of a mystery and the thrilling formal inventiveness of the great epistolary novels. Jonathon Bender's magical letters to the world that never wrote to him are at once whimsical, anguished, funny, utterly engaging and, finally, unforgettable."

— Maud Casey

Tyrant Books

676A 9th Ave. #153, New York 10036

isbn# 978-0-615-43046-1

First Tyrant Books Edition, 2011

First published in Great Britain in 2005 by
Fourth Estate

The author would like to thank the editors of *New York Tyrant, Prairie Schooner, Open City, Unsaid, LitRag, Sleeping Fish, Avatar Review, Mud Luscious, Necessary Fiction, Whiskey Island,* and *The Collagist* where excepts of the novel first appeared, often in a different form.

A different version of this book was previously published in other countries under the title *How Much of Us There Was.*

Designed by Ryan P Kirby
Cover art by Shelton Walsmith and
The Flying Chabowskis
Author photo: Rachel Bradley
www.nytyrantbooks.com   www.michael-kimball.com

Us

Michael Kimball

TYRANT BOOKS

For my grandparents,
Kenneth and Gertrude Oliver.

And for my wife, Tita.

We seemed to decay at night. There were little sheets
of our skin in our bed every morning.

Her Husband

It was so late in our lives.

His Wife

I blacked out and fell down. I hit my head on the floor
and forgot my wife and myself for a while.

My Grandfather Oliver

I wasn't me anymore either.

Michael Kimball

PART ONE

PART TWO

PART ONE

How My Wife Would Not Wake Up

Our bed was shaking and it woke me up afraid. My wife didn't wake up and her body seemed to keep seizing up. That stopped and her body dropped back down flat on our bed again. She let one long breath out and then stopped moving and breathing. She looked as if she were sleeping again, but she wouldn't wake up.

I turned the bedroom light on, but that didn't wake her up. I tried to shake her some more, but that didn't wake her up either. I laid her shoulders back down on our bed and her head back down on her pillow. I picked her glass of water up from her bedside table and opened her mouth up and tipped a little water in, but she didn't swallow it. I pulled her eyelids up, but her eyes didn't look back at me, and her eyelids closed up again when I let go of them.

I picked the telephone up to call for somebody to come to help me get my wife up. I covered my wife up with the bedcovers to keep her warm. I pulled the bedcovers up to her neck. I brushed her hair back away from her face with my hand and touched her cheek. I held my fingers under her nose and over her mouth. I couldn't feel any breath coming out of her anymore. I held onto her nose and tried to breathe some of my breath into her mouth. There didn't seem to be enough air inside of me to get her to breathe.

I was afraid to leave my wife in our bed, but I was also afraid that the ambulance might not find our house. I walked out of our bedroom, down the hall-way, and up into the front of our house. I turned all of the lights in all of the front rooms of our house on. I opened the front door up, stood in the doorway, and turned the light on the front porch on too. I wanted them to know that it was our house and us that needed them.

How They Helped My Wife to Breathe

They came inside our house to take my wife away from me and to the hospital. They banged their way through the front door and into the living room. One of them carried an oxygen tank, an oxygen mask, and a metal box that had drawers inside it that folded up and out when he opened it up. The other one of them rolled a metal gurney inside our house that had folding legs under it and a flat board tied down on top of it. He rolled it inside our house, down the hallway, and into our bedroom. They set everything that they had with them down around our bed and my wife and they checked to see if she were still alive.

One of them pulled the bedcovers down off her and straightened her nightgown out. He touched her neck and held onto her wrist. He listened to her chest for her heart. He pulled her eyelids up, opened her mouth up, and looked inside her mouth and into her eyes with a tiny flashlight. He put his ear down over her mouth and close to her nose to see if he could hear or feel her breathing.

The other one got the oxygen tank out, placed the oxygen mask over her face, and turned the oxygen tank on. My wife seemed to take a deep breath in and stay alive. They rolled her over onto her one side and placed the flat board on top of our bed where her body had been. They rolled her back down onto the flat board, lifted her up, and placed the flat board and her back down on the metal gurney.

My wife looked so light in their arms. I wanted to lift her up too.

They pulled the gurney blanket up to her neck to cover her up, but they left her arms out. It looked as if she were holding them out to me.

One of them moved me out of the way with his arm. They both rolled the metal gurney with my wife on top of it out of our bedroom, back down the hallway, and out the front door. They carried her down the front steps, rolled her down the front walk, and lifted her up into the back of the ambulance.

I followed them out of our house and down the front walk, but I could not have climbed up into the back of that ambulance. They would have had to lift me up into it too.

One of them climbed up into the back of the ambulance with my wife and the other one pushed the two back doors closed and climbed up into the front. He told me to follow them to the hospital and he drove away from me with my wife. They left me out there on the sidewalk in front of our house. They left me out there in the nighttime with their ambulance lights flashing red all around me. They didn't turn their siren on.

I went back inside our house and then back out through the back door to the driveway. I backed our car out of the driveway and drove away after the ambulance. I could see the red lights flashing up ahead of me and flashing high up on the sides of the buildings and the tops of the trees that lined the streets. The streetlights blinked off and on and off and on all the way to the hospital. I followed the blinking and the flashing lights after my wife. I didn't want to lose the ambulance.

I didn't want to lose my wife. I wanted to see my wife lying down in a hospital bed. I wanted to see my wife breathing again. I wanted to see her get up out of bed again. I wanted to see her get up out of our bed again. I wanted my wife to come back home and live there with me again.

How the People at the Hospital Couldn't Find My Wife

I parked our car next to the emergency room entrance and left the engine on. I thought that might somehow help keep my wife alive. The ambulance that had had my wife inside it was parked there too, but there weren't any people inside it anymore. The hood of the ambulance was still warm and it made me think that my wife must still be alive.

I went through the emergency room's sliding glass doors to look for the two people who had carried my wife out of our house and driven her to the hospital, but I couldn't find them or the metal gurney that had my wife on it. I asked the people at the information desk where my wife was, but they couldn't find out what bed or room she was in. The people at the admissions desk didn't know if she had been admitted yet.

They all looked for her by her first name and by her last name, but none of them had her name in their computers or on any of their clipboards. The admissions people said that she might be inside the hospital even though she wasn't in the computer yet. They didn't have anybody who had our last name.

I went to other departments in other parts of the hospital. I asked for my wife at other desks on other floors of the hospital. I gave everybody her name and I gave them my name too. I tried to describe what she looked like, but none of them had seen a woman who looked like what I said.

I walked along the long hallways looking for her on any metal gurney that I found. I looked through hospital rooms. I looked through open doors and opened doors that were closed. I called her name up and down the hallways and through the doorways and behind those curtains that circle hospital beds, but she couldn't hear me or couldn't answer me and I couldn't find her.

The hallways and the hospital rooms were filled with people who weren't my wife. There were people sitting down in their wheelchairs and other people walking behind them pushing them. There were people trying to walk with their IV bags even though they couldn't really lift their feet up off the floor.

There were people inside the hospital rooms who were propped up in their hospital beds and watching the television up on the wall. Some of them were eating food off trays and some of them had to have their food spooned into their mouths by other people who could stand up and move their arms. Some of the hospital rooms were quiet with machines and with somebody dying in the hospital bed. Some of the people didn't move or look at me when I looked inside their hospital room at them. They were dying in different ways and at different speeds.

There were other people who looked back at me as if they were expecting me. They looked almost hopeful when I looked inside their hospital room at them. They were mostly probably waiting for somebody to come to see them. They were probably waiting for a doctor or a nurse or maybe they were waiting for a husband or a wife.

I wasn't a doctor or a nurse who could help them get any better or tell them that they were ready to go home. I didn't have any pills or needles or bandages or salve. I didn't have any instruments to heal them. I didn't know what the numbers or beeps or counts on any of the machines were supposed to mean. I didn't understand their kind of medical pain. I couldn't offer any comfort to them or say anything to them to make them feel any better. I couldn't somehow help them. I didn't bring them any flowers or a get well card. I didn't bring them a bathrobe or anything else from home. I wasn't their husband or father or brother or son or even their friend and none of them were my wife.

Everybody who I found anywhere inside the hospital was still alive, so I thought that my wife must be too. I went back down to the emergency room to look for her. I found the ambulance driver and the one who rode inside the back of the ambulance with my wife, but they didn't have my wife with them anymore.

I went back outside to find our car. It was still parked there. Nobody had moved it or towed it away and nobody had turned the engine off either. I saw the exhaust coming out of the exhaust pipe of our car and it made me think that my wife must still be breathing somewhere back up inside that hospital.

The Dying Woman Who Looked Smaller and Older Than My Wife

I waited in the hospital lobby until I heard them call my name over the hospital intercom. They called my name again and it sounded as if my wife were calling me from another room from somewhere inside our house. Her voice was sort of fuzzy and distorted, but she was calling me back up into the hospital. I went back up to the floor and to the desk that I thought she said and the woman there said that they had a woman there who might be my wife.

She walked me down a hallway and into a hospital room. She took me past an empty hospital bed, behind a curtain, and past a bank of machines. They had most of her body covered up with sheets and blankets and she seemed too small to be my wife. Her head was propped up with a pillow and they had laid her hair out on it, but her hair looked too thin and too gray to be my wife's hair. Her arms were laid outside the sheets and the blankets and her skin seemed to be colored with the colored lights from the machines that seemed to be keeping her alive. Her eyes were closed and another part of her face was covered up with an oxygen mask. She didn't look like my wife like that, but I had never seen my wife dying before that night and I didn't know what it was going to look like.

How Much of Her Still Worked

The nurse handed me the clipboard with the forms on it and sat me down in a chair next to my wife's hospital bed. There were other doctors and other nurses inside the hospital room. They seemed to be taking some kind of care of my wife, but they all also seemed to be waiting for me to fill all those forms out before they did anything else for her.

I wrote my wife's name down while they watched over my wife and me. I gave them our address and her birthday and her social security number. I skimmed over the medical history list. I checked asthma and cancer, allergies to certain medications, and recent surgery. I filled all the blanks in. I wrote my name in for her emergency contact and I signed a line that said that they could treat her to keep her alive. I gave them my insurance card, my credit card, my driver's license, and another card with my name and picture on it.

One of the nurses took the clipboard with the forms on it and the cards that I gave her and left some charts with my wife's name on them on another clipboard in a plastic holder at the end of her hospital bed. Another nurse picked the clipboard back up, took my wife's temperature and then her pulse, and then wrote them down on one of the charts. Another nurse measured her blood pressure and how much my wife could breathe in without the machine on and then she turned the machine back on and wrote those things down too.

They found a vein in my wife's arm so that they could hook an IV up to it and drip the bags of fluid into her. They said that the IV might wake my wife up, but it didn't stop her from sleeping either.

They found another vein in my wife's other arm and took some blood out of it. They said they needed to check her blood to see what was in it. They wanted to know if her blood had enough sugar and enough minerals in it. They said that they would know if her kidneys and her liver still worked.

One of the nurses took the blood away for the tests and then two other hospital workers came in and took my wife away for other tests. They rolled her out of her hospital room and down the hallway on her metal gurney with her IV bag and her respirator alongside her. They were going to test her heart and also her brain. They were trying to find out how much of her still worked.

Why I Stayed Awake

My wife wasn't very alive then. She couldn't keep herself alive, but there were doctors and nurses who could. There were machines that could feed her and that could help her lungs to breathe and her heart to beat. But one of the doctors told me that since her eyes didn't open, and she didn't seem to hear anything that he said to her or move any on her own, that my wife probably wouldn't be alive without the machines and that she might not be alive in the morning with them.

I felt as if I were already in mourning. I looked at the nurse and the nurse put her head down. I looked back at the doctor and the doctor looked back down at the charts on the clipboard in his hands. I looked away too. I tried not to cry. I lifted my hand up to my face and held onto my jaw so that it wouldn't shake. I thought that they might not leave me alone with my wife if I started to cry.

The doctor said something else and the nurse did too. I couldn't hear them anymore, but I nodded at them both. I didn't say anything more. I kept looking at my wife.

They didn't move for a long time. They were quiet too. Then the nurse said that she would come back to check on my wife. The doctor left the clipboard in the plastic holder at the end of the hospital bed. He left the hospital room and the nurse did too.

They left me there even though I wasn't supposed to stay inside the hospital room with my wife. It was too late and the hours weren't right, but they left me sitting down in the visitor's chair next to my wife's hospital bed.

I watched my wife try to stay alive for that night. I turned the visitor's chair so that I was facing my wife's face, but she didn't open her eyes up to look back at me. It didn't look easy for her to breathe even though she had all those machines trying to help her to do it.

The machines and the wires made her look so tired. I was tired too. I wanted to get into the hospital bed with my wife and go back to sleep with her. I wanted to sleep her sleep with her.

The nurse who kept checking to see if my wife were still alive kept me up through the night. She brought me a pillow and a blanket and I made a kind of sitting bed in my visitor's chair. I still didn't sleep. I thought that it might help my wife to stay alive if I stayed awake. I thought that she might open her eyes up if I kept looking at her. I turned the lights on inside her hospital room so that she might think that it was morning and might wake up.

How I Tried to Make It
More of a Morning for My Wife

I had fallen asleep, but my wife hadn't died. I had woken up, but my wife hadn't woken up too. She hadn't moved either.

I whispered into her ear that it was morning, but she didn't seem to hear me. I nudged her at her shoulder and touched her upper arm, but she still didn't open her eyes up, so I opened the blinds on the windows up. I turned her head to face the light coming in through the windows.

I whistled bird sounds, but she didn't open her eyes up or put a pillow over her ear or turn her face away or roll over away from the light. My wife hadn't shifted her body since she had been in that hospital bed. She hadn't kicked the bedcovers off her legs and her feet or pushed the pillow onto the floor. She hadn't tossed or kicked or turned over in her sleep like she did when she would sleep in our bed at home.

She didn't wake up for the morning as she had on every other day of our marriage, but we ate breakfast together that day anyway. One of the nurses brought a tray of food into the hospital room and placed it on top of the table that swung over the hospital bed. I told the nurse that my wife couldn't eat or drink or swallow or chew, but the nurse didn't take the tray of food away when she left the hospital room.

The nurse came back in with an IV bag for my wife. She hung the IV bag up on the IV stand and made sure that the drips worked. I watched the IV bag drip for a while before I took the tray of food off the table and set it on my lap and started to eat too.

We ate breakfast together, but it still wasn't morning for my wife, so I tried to make it into more of a morning. I decided to wash up. I pushed myself up out of that chair and stood up. The blood seemed to rush out of my head and I couldn't really breathe right. I had to use that chair's armrests to hold myself up. I was bent over until I got my breath back. I stood up straight again and my head cleared up.

I took my hat off and left it on top of the back of that chair. I took my jacket off and hung it around the shoulders of that chair. I pulled the sleeves of the jacket around to the front of that chair and left them resting on its armrests. I wanted to make it look as if I were sitting there, or at least make it seem as if I were nearby, if my wife woke up.

I didn't want her to wake up without me there with her. I didn't want her to be awake and alone at the same time.

I went into the bathroom inside her hospital room to take as much of a bath or a shower as I could. I smelled like sleep and I wanted to wash the sleep off me. I took my clothes off and hung them up on the back of the bathroom door and laid them out on all the handles and bars that are supposed to help people get up or stand up inside a hospital bathroom. I turned the water faucet on and washed myself off with wet paper towels. I dried myself off with dry paper towels, but it didn't really make me feel clean. I felt dry and tired. I felt as if I had shrunk.

I turned my underwear and my undershirt and my socks inside out. I wanted to have the clean side of them touching my skin when I put them back on. I shook the rest of my clothes out. I tried to get the sleep off them too. I tried to move some air through them too.

I got dressed again, but my clothes felt sticky and thick on me. It was difficult to move in them. My pants could almost stand up on their cuffs on their own and my shirt seemed to keep its own shape around my shoulders. My clothes looked stiff and wrinkled and so did I. But my clothes also helped me stand up. I needed something else to hold me up.

I stood over the bathroom sink and looked at myself in the bathroom mirror. I looked smaller and older too. I turned the water faucet back on and splashed water on my hair and on my face. I pushed my hair down with my hands and combed it back with my fingers. I wet one of my fingers again and brushed my teeth with it until my teeth felt smooth to my tongue.

I straightened myself back up and stood back away from the bathroom sink and the bathroom mirror. I tried to straighten my clothes out some more, but they didn't seem to fit right anymore. My clothes and everything else seemed bigger than me. I tucked my shirt further down into my pants and tightened my belt a notch. I took a long breath in and tried to fill my clothes out with myself. I was going to need all of me for this morning.

The Small Things that I Asked Her For

The doctors and the nurses monitored her lungs and her heart and her brain. They kept checking her to see if she would open her eyes up or respond in any way to anything they said. They kept checking her for her blood pressure and for how much oxygen her lungs could process. They kept testing her for how much blood was going into and out of her brain and for how much pressure there was on it. They kept measuring parts of my wife so that they could find out how much she was alive.

The doctor told me that the numbers were getting worse and that my wife wasn't getting any better. There wasn't enough oxygen going into or out of her lungs or enough blood moving through her brain and the doctor told me that my wife probably wouldn't gain consciousness again.

But I thought that there had to be something that would wake her up again. I thought about snoring or making some other kind of noise from our sleep. I thought about kissing her on the forehead or on the cheek. I wanted the telephone to ring or for somebody to knock on the door to her hospital room. I wanted her to have a nightmare or even insomnia. I wanted the alarm on the alarm clock to go off. I wanted it to be morning again.

The doctor started talking about unhooking the IVs and unplugging the machines, but I didn't want them to undo any of her treatment. I wanted them to do more of anything that might make her wake up, but the doctor told me that they couldn't do anything else medical for her. The doctor said that we had to wait for her to be more conscious before they could do anything else for her.

The doctor told me that if she did anything again that she would be able to hear again first. He told me to talk to her. He told me to ask her for small things.

I asked her to open her eyes back up. I asked her to move her eyes back and forth under her eyelids so that her eyelids would tremble some. I asked her to smile or move her lips even a little bit. I watched her eyes and her lips for a twitch or for any other kind of change in the way that her face looked. I held onto her hand and asked her to move her fingers, but she didn't move them or seem to touch my hand back. I asked her if the bruises on her arms from the needles and the tubes hurt.

I told her that the skin on her hands was soft and that I liked the age spots on the backs of her hands. I told her that she had a soft dress with polka dots on it that she liked to wear. I told her about where we met and about the hospital room where we were then. I told her that she was lying down in a hospital bed and wearing a hospital gown that she probably would not like. I told her that she probably would not like the hospital room either. I told her that we should go home soon.

My wife didn't say anything back or seem to hear anything that I said to her. The doctor told me that I should go home and come back with some things from home that would remind my wife of being at home. The nurse told me that I should go home for a change of clothes for my wife and for myself. The nurse told me that I should take a shower and get some rest and come back fresh. The nurse told me that I should pack up enough clothes so that I could stay at the hospital for a while.

I was afraid to go back home and pack up our clothes. I was afraid that my wife might die if I did not stay there with her. I felt as if I were somehow keeping my wife alive by being there with her.

How I Tried to Drive Myself Home

My legs felt heavy and sleepy when I tried to stand up to walk out of her hospital room. I stumbled a couple of steps forward toward my wife. I had to stop and hold myself up over her hospital bed with my arms. My back tingled and spasmed. I couldn't feel the back of my head. I needed help to breathe too.

I waited until I had enough breath to talk. I leaned over her in her hospital bed and whispered into her ear. I told her to wait for me to come back to see her. I kissed each of her eyelids and touched her hair and her ear and her cheek.

I walked along the side and the foot of her hospital bed with my arm holding onto the edge of it to help hold me up. I straightened my back up and held my head up. I walked away from her hospital bed, past the empty hospital bed, to the doorway and out of her hospital room.

It was so hard for me to walk out of that room. I didn't know how she was going to get up out of her hospital bed and leave too.

I stopped outside the doorway. The hallway was so much brighter than her hospital room was that I had to close my eyes. I turned around to look back inside her hospital room at her, but it was already too dark inside there for me to see my wife anymore.

I walked away down the hallway, got on the elevator going down, and went down to the hospital lobby. I got my legs back under me and walked through the sliding glass doors and out into the parking lot. I had parked our car under one of those tall lamps out in the parking lot, but it had been so many days since then that I couldn't remember where or which one.

I looked up at the different lamps and watched the insects that were flying around the lights up there. I walked from lamp to lamp through the parking lot until I found our car. I opened the car door up and started to get inside, but my body wouldn't bend enough for me to get into it. I held myself up with the car door and sat down sideways into our car. I backed myself into the driver's seat and lifted my legs up into our car with the rest of me. I was too tired to drive and I was almost out of gas, but I thought I had enough to get me back home.

I tried to drive home, but I couldn't keep my eyes open. I kept falling asleep and then waking up afraid. I kept pulling over to the curb to sleep, but I could never sleep once our car was parked there. I would start driving back home again. I would pull back out into the street and then wake up blocks later. There seemed to be two grooves worn down into the street that seemed to keep the left set of tires and the right set of tires rolling me back toward home. I didn't even need to hold onto the steering wheel and I was almost back home.

I drove by the front of our house and saw that I had left all the lights at the front of our house on. It made me think of the lights on my wife's machines inside her hospital room and it made it look as if some-body were at home and living inside our house.

I drove around to the side of our house, drove back up the driveway, and parked our car there. I had left the front door and the back door open too. I walked into our house and down the hallway and into our bedroom. Our bed was still unmade and the shape of my wife was still marked out in the pillows and the blankets and the sheets.

I walked up and down the hallway and through the rooms of our house—our bedroom, the bathroom, the spare bedroom, the guestroom, the other bathroom, the study, the kitchen, the dining room, and the living room – but I knew that I wasn't going to find my wife inside any of those rooms.

I didn't know what to do without her there at home with me. I held onto my head, but my hair was dirty and it was slick. My skin itched too and my clothes felt sticky on my skin and kind of hard. I took my clothes off and let them fall down my body and into a pile of dirty laundry around me.

I walked into the bathroom, turned the hot water and the cold water in the shower on, got into the shower, and pulled the shower curtain along the length of the bathtub. The water hurt and the shower made me tired. My skin tingled and my back spasmed some more. My eyelids got heavy and covered up most of my eyes too.

I needed to go to sleep too. I wanted to lie down in bed with my wife and go back to sleep with her so that both of us could wake up again. I fixed the pillow on her side of our bed. I fixed the sheets and the blankets and pulled them up over where she would have been sleeping if she would have been there with me.

I got into my side of our bed and lay my head down and my cheek deep into the pillow. I turned over so that I was facing her part of our bed. I reached my arm out to hold onto the place where she usually was and I kept thinking that we would both be sleeping and that we might see each other in our sleep.

Come Back to Sleep with Me

I have been hoping you would come back to sleep with me. I didn't mean to keep you up so long. I didn't mean to make you so tired too. I have been too tired to wake up yet, but I will wake up soon. You should too. I want you to wake up so you can come back to the hospital and come back up to me. Bring my hairbrush with you when you come back up to me. Bring my slippers with you too. Wake back up and come back up and I will wake up too.

The Things that I Brought Her from Our House

It was still nighttime outside when I woke up. I couldn't remember where I was in the dark. My wife wasn't in our bed with me and I couldn't remember where she was even though she had just been talking with me. I rolled over and looked at her empty side of our bed. I remembered her hospital bed where she was and how she was laid out in it.

I turned the bedside light on the bedside table on and looked at the date on my watch. I had been asleep for too long too. I called the hospital up with the telephone on the bedside table, but my wife hadn't died or woken up yet.

I got up out of bed and went into the kitchen. I wanted to eat until I was so full that the food pushed how I felt out of my stomach. I opened the refrigerator door up, but there was so much food inside the refrigerator that had gotten old and started to rot. The blood had drained out of a package of steaks and turned the meat a gray color. The milk was lumpy and sour and had this crusty skin floating on it. The bread had a spotty mold growing on its crust and the vegetables in the crisper had gotten soft and lost their color too.

I closed the refrigerator door and filled a water glass up from the faucet tap, but even the water tasted old and flat. I put the water glass down into the kitchen sink and saw the bananas on the countertop. They had brown age spots on them and little flies flying around them, but I couldn't throw any of that rotten food away. I didn't want my wife to die.

I wanted to go back to the hospital. I wanted to be with her even if she couldn't be with me. I pulled two suitcases out of the closet and laid them out on our bed. I packed one suitcase up for her and the other one up for me. We didn't live that far away from the hospital, but we were both going to be away from home for a while. I packed up my toiletry bag up, along with enough days of clothes for me to change into until she got better or died.

I packed clothes up for her too—nightgowns and a housecoat, slippers and almost her whole drawer of underclothes. I packed clothes up that she could wear out of the hospital too. I packed the things on her bedside table up—an alarm clock, a reading lamp, the book she was reading, her reading glasses, and her glass for water. I packed her make-up kit up, which had the things for her to fix her hair up with inside it—a hand mirror, her good hairbrush, and a can of hairspray.

I packed her pillow up along with a blanket from our bed. I brought other things from our house for her too. I cut flowers from the front garden and put them in water so that they looked as if they were still alive. I picked out some music that she liked and I brought back other sounds from our house for her too.

I recorded the sound of the water running from the kitchen and the bathroom faucets. I recorded the sound of the latches from when I opened and closed the doors on the cupboards. I recorded the furnace heating up, the water heater coming on, the dishwasher washing dishes, and the washing machine washing clothes and the dryer drying them. I put the tape recorder on the wood floors and walked over them where they creaked. I recorded the sound of our house settling on its foundation at night. I recorded the back door closing shut and my shoes walking over the gravel in the driveway.

I set the tape recorder on top of our car and opened the trunk up, packed the suitcases in it, and closed the trunk back up. I opened our car up and set the tape recorder on the seat next to me. I closed our car, started it up, and drove everything that I had with me back to her.

How I Unpacked the Suitcases
in Her Hospital Room

I drove back to the hospital in the dark, but it was almost morning. People were starting to wake up and get up and turn the lights on in the bedrooms and the bathrooms and the kitchens of their houses. There were more and more cars with their headlights on driving up and down the streets on my way back to the hospital.

The hospital parking lot was still lit up with those tall lamps. They gave off a false morning light for that soft hospital world.

There were a lot of people walking both toward and away from the hospital and their cars. There was a change of shifts at the hospital. There were doctors and nurses and other hospital workers going home to go to sleep and even more of them who had already gotten up to come back to work.

There were also all of us people who walked back and forth between the hospital and the parking lot before and after visiting hours. We looked different than the people who worked at the hospital. We were carrying things—flowers and clothes and books and food—and many of us were looking up at a particular floor of the hospital to see if the light in a particular window were on.

We nodded our heads to each other or said hello in some other quiet way. Our hair was brushed or combed. Our clothes looked neat and seemed clean. We looked as if we had slept but were still tired. We looked anxious and walked fast. We were all hurrying into the hospital to see if there had been any change in our husband or wife or mother or father or son or daughter. We wanted to know if anything had happened to them while we were at home or asleep. We wanted to get up to their hospital room before they woke up or before they died.

I carried our two suitcases into the hospital through the sliding glass doors, through the lobby, and waited for the elevator to take me back up to my wife. There were other people waiting for the elevator with me and all of us looked old. It could have been any one of us dying too.

We rode the elevator up together, but we got off at different floors. There were different floors for heart attacks and for strokes. There were different floors for organ transplants and for the cancer ward. I got off the elevator at the floor for the intensive care unit. The elevator's mechanical doors opened up onto a hallway that looked so bright that it looked as if the sun were coming up inside.

I picked our two suitcases up and carried them down the hallway toward her hospital room. I pushed the door to her hospital room open, but I couldn't really see through the darkness inside there. It seemed as if it were nighttime all the time in that hospital room.

I set our two suitcases down inside the doorway and looked down through the low light toward her hospital bed. My wife was still there, but she just looked like a blanketed shape. My eyes adjusted to the darkness enough for me to see her face, but I couldn't see that anything had changed in her face. All of the machines and the IVs were all the same as they had been when I had left. My wife was still alive, but she was still asleep.

I told her that we had seen each other in our sleep and that she had told me to come back to her. I told her that I wanted her to come back to me too. I told her that it was almost morning and that she should wake up so that we could eat breakfast together again.

I told her that I had brought her some clean clothes so that she could change her clothes and we could go back home. I told her that I had brought her some flowers for her. I asked her if she wanted me to brush her hair for her. I asked her which one of her nightgowns she wanted to wear and if she wanted to change her underwear and if she wanted to wear her housecoat over everything.

I didn't know what else to tell her or to say. I looked away from her. I looked down at the floor and then I looked back up at her face and her face had changed. Her eyebrows were somehow a little higher on her face. It looked as if she were trying to pull her eyelids up so that she could open her eyes up to look at me. Or maybe she was asking me why I had stopped talking. Or maybe she was asking me where she was and why she was there.

I answered her questions back. I told her that she was in a hospital bed and that I was standing next to it. I told her that she had had a seizure in our bed at home and that she had been sleeping ever since then.

I told her that they were feeding her through IVs and that she was feeding herself with sleep. I told her that I was going to unpack our two suitcases so that I could stay there with her.

I set our two suitcases down on the empty hospital bed next to her hospital bed and opened them up. I let the locks snap open and it sounded as if we were on vacation. I unpacked our changes of clothes and put them away in a little set of dresser drawers that was next to her hospital bed. I laid a nightgown and the housecoat out over the armrest of the visitor's chair. I set her slippers down under her hospital bed. I set the reading lamp, the book she was reading, and her reading glasses out on the bedside table. I put her make-up kit inside the bathroom. I set the flowers from our front garden on the windowsill.

I lifted the back of her head up off her hospital pillow and slid her pillow from home back under her head. I unpacked the blanket, unfolded it, and laid it out on top of the other blankets that covered my wife up. I got the alarm clock out and plugged it into a wall socket. It blinked the time off and on and I set the time and set the alarm. It was almost morning and she was almost awake. I wanted to see if this would wake her the rest of the way up.

The Other Woman Who They Put
in the Other Hospital Bed

There were two hospital workers who rolled a metal gurney with another woman on top of it into my wife's hospital room. The doctors and the nurses rolled her machines and her IVs in after her and made sure that everything was plugged into the wall sockets and turned on and working right. The two hospital workers took what must have been a few of her things out of a plastic bag that was on the metal gurney and laid them out on her bedside table. One of the doctors looked at the machines, wrote some things down on her medical charts, left them in the plastic holder at the end of her hospital bed, and left the hospital room along with the rest of the doctors and the nurses.

Another hospital worker brought some flowers into that hospital room for that other woman. He left them on the table at the end of her hospital bed and then he left too.

There were nurses who visited the hospital room throughout the day to check on the machines and the IVs and to fill out the medical charts for both of the women in both of the hospital beds. Other hospital workers brought in trays of food, but these seemed to be for me since nobody else inside that hospital room could eat any food that wasn't dripping from IV bags and flowing through tubes.

Nobody else came into that hospital room for that other woman until one of her machines went into a long beep. It sounded like an alarm clock going off and the doctors and the nurses all came back into that hospital room. That other woman in that other hospital bed was dying, but they were trying to keep her alive too.

They checked her IV lines and her eyes. They tapped on the glass of the machines and they checked the plugs of the machines at the outlets. They checked her blood pressure and her heart rate. They wheeled another machine into the hospital room and shocked her with paddles on her chest that made her body seize up off her hospital bed. They pressed down on her chest with their hands and pushed the air out of her lungs. They pulled her jaw down and her mouth open and held onto her nose. They pushed air back into her mouth and her lungs with their mouths and their lungs and then let the air rise back up out of her.

That other woman wasn't really doing anything anymore and the doctors and the nurses stopped doing anything else to her. They looked at each other and looked down at the floor. One of the nurses looked over at my wife and me and walked over to pull the curtain that separated their two hospital beds into alive and dead sides across that hospital room.

I heard all the doctors and all the nurses leave the hospital room and I heard the door being eased shut. I pulled the curtain back and saw that they had left that other woman's body in that other hospital bed. I thought that she might still be alive, but they had turned off and unplugged all her machines. There weren't any beeps or numbers or lights anymore.

Two more hospital workers came back for that other woman's body. They pulled the sheets all the way down off her hospital bed so that they could pick her up. One of them picked her body up under the arms and the other one picked it up around the ankles. They lifted her body up off the hospital bed and set it down inside a long bag that they had laid open on a metal gurney. They tucked her feet into the foot of the bag and they pulled the top of the bag up around her shoulders and the sides of the bag up around her arms. They zipped the bag up and rolled the metal gurney and the bag with her body inside it out of that hospital room and away down the hallway.

One of them came back to pick up the few other things that she had with her—some worn clothes, some old magazines, some wilted flowers, and a toiletry bag. He gathered everything up, put all of it inside a plastic garbage bag, and tied the top of the garbage bag into a knot. He stripped the pillowcases off the pillows and the blankets and the sheets off the hospital bed. He cleared the food tray away and wiped the table down where the tray had been. He wiped the bedside table and the handles on the sides of the bed down too.

He made that hospital bed back up and pulled the side handles back up, but they didn't put anybody else back in that hospital bed. They were waiting to see if my wife were going to wake up and get up out of her hospital bed without dying too.

How I Moved into Her Hospital Room

I moved into my wife's hospital room with her. I lived with her inside her hospital room and ate hospital food. I took my baths inside that hospital room's bathroom and changed my clothes inside there too. I slept in the empty hospital bed next to her hospital bed and I kept the curtain that separated our two hospital beds pulled back so that there wasn't anything else between us but her sleep.

The nurses who came into the hospital room to check on my wife started to check on me too. They would touch my shoulder to wake me up to let me know that they were there and they would sometimes bring me an extra tray of hospital food or the things that other people didn't eat or drink—those little boxes of cereal, a cup of crushed ice, a little bottle of apple juice, or a small bowl of jello with fruit inside it that was wrapped up in plastic. I didn't have to go down to the hospital cafeteria to eat. I didn't have to leave that hospital room or my wife.

The nurses let me help them with my wife too. I would hold onto my wife's body for them when they would move her so that she wouldn't get any bedsores. I would hold her body up on one side when they rolled her back and forth to change the sheets or change her clothes. They would leave me a bowl of soapy water and a hand sponge and a hand towel so that I could give my wife a sponge bath and then dry her off.

I was more of a husband when I could do these things for my wife. But my wife had started to shrink. The clothes that we changed her into were too big on her and she looked smaller and more wrinkled in them. Her chest seemed to sink in. She was breathing too much of herself out and not enough back in.

The nurses showed me how to move my wife's arms and her legs for her. I started every morning with her arms. I held onto her hands, bent her arms at the elbows, and then straightened them back out. I pulled her arms out away from her body, raised them up over her shoulders, and then brought them back down to her sides. I moved her hands back and forth at the wrist. I bent her fingers back and then curled them back in so that she would be able to hold something in her hands again. I opened her hands back up and put my hands into them. I held onto her hands to see if she could hold my hands back yet.

I lifted her leg up at her ankle and then bent her leg in at the knee. I bent her ankles up and down and back and forth. I wanted her to be able to stand up and not wobble or fall down when she woke up and could stand up and I wanted her to be able to walk again.

I got onto the hospital bed with her and pulled her upper body up until she was sitting up. I pulled her eyelids up with my thumb so that she would be able to open her eyes up again. I turned her head to each side so that she could look out through the door-way and then look out through the window. I opened her mouth up at her jaw so that she would be ready to talk again after she woke up again.

I whispered things into her ears so that she would remember how to talk and remember me and the things that we did together. I would say that we were going for a walk when I moved her legs and I would say that we were holding hands when I held onto her hands. I would tell her that she was taking a bath in our bathtub. I would tell her that she was sitting up in a chair or looking out the window or brushing her hair.

I would play the tape with the sounds from our house on it for her. I would tell her that she was getting a glass of water from the kitchen sink or that we were making lunch. I would tell her that the door latch and the sound of the door closing was the sound of her coming home. I would tell her that we had put everything down and that we were walking back down the hallway to our bedroom and that we were going back to bed and back to sleep.

How My Wife Started to Move Again

My wife didn't wake up again for so many more days, but the way that she slept started to get restless. She started to move a little bit. Sometimes her body shifted during the nighttime. Sometimes I saw that her arms and her hands or her legs had moved some in the morning. One afternoon I watched her fingers twitch and on another day I watched her toes curl and uncurl under her bedcovers. Sometimes her eyelids would flutter a little bit and I would go to the end of her hospital bed and stand there so that she would see me if she woke up and opened her eyes up.

How We Talked with Our Eyes
and Our Hands

I woke up and she had woken up too. She had
opened her eyes up, but she couldn't turn her head
to look at me in the other hospital bed. I got up and
went around to the end of her hospital bed so that she
could see me too.

My wife looked so much brighter with her
eyes open. She looked so much more alive when she
was looking back at me. I held onto her feet with my
hands and she pushed her toes against them. She
must have been smiling under that oxygen mask, but
I didn't know what to say to her, and she couldn't talk
again yet.

But we talked with our eyes and our hands. She lifted some of her fingers up enough so that it felt as if she were reaching for me. I walked over to the side of her hospital bed and closer to her arms. I lifted her arms up for her and put myself in them. I put my hands and my arms around her too.

I only lifted myself back up away from her so that we could look at each other again. She looked at me and then looked down her face at the oxygen mask. I thought that she wanted to say something to me so I lifted the oxygen mask up and pulled it up over her head, but she just wanted to breathe with her nose and her mouth and her lungs. But I was afraid that she might stop breathing deep enough into herself without the machine, so I pushed the button that called the doctors and the nurses into her hospital room.

They asked my wife who she was and where she was and what day and month and year it was. My wife knew her name, that she was in a hospital, and the year that she was living in. But she didn't know the day and she thought that it was the month before the one that we were living in.

They looked into her eyes and her ears with a tiny flashlight. They asked her to breathe in, but she couldn't get much air into her lungs. It was enough to keep her alive.

They asked her to move her fingers and her toes and she did. But she couldn't lift her arms and her legs up off her hospital bed. She couldn't lift her head up off the pillow.

They wanted to see if she could drink or swallow, but she couldn't hold onto the cup of water or the pill that was supposed to keep her from having any more seizures. A nurse set the pill on my wife's tongue and tipped some water from the cup into her mouth so that she could swallow it. Another nurse brought in a tray of soft food to see what else my wife could eat.

They fed her spoonfuls of chicken broth, oatmeal, and jello. They shook little clumps of ice chips into her mouth from a plastic cup and they put a straw into a little bottle of apple juice and the straw into her mouth to see if she could draw the apple juice out of the bottle. My wife could eat and drink enough that they could unhook the IVs and pull her tubes out, but somebody else was going to have to feed her and she needed to move more than she could then before we could go back home again.

The Small Ways that She Got Better

I still had to move her arms and her legs for her so that they would still work when she could move them again for herself. I had to hold onto the cup of water or the bottle of apple juice, but she could put the straw into her mouth so that she could drink. She could hold onto a spoon, but she couldn't move it to her mouth without spilling the food.

The spoon trembled in my hand too. We were both afraid of her dying.

There were so many small ways that my wife started to get better than she had been. She moved from eating soft food to solid food and to going to the bathroom inside the bathroom instead of into a bedpan or through tubes. She started to smile with both sides of her mouth and then with her whole face. She started to move all her fingers and both her thumbs. She could lift her arms up and reach her hands out and touch me with them.

She could sit up in bed again and then she could get out of her hospital bed. She couldn't stand up with just her legs, but she could hold herself up with her arms. She could stand up with her walker before she could walk again, and then she could walk back and forth between her hospital bed and the bathroom, and then between the nurse's station and her hospital room, and then all the way around the floor of the hospital. She could walk and eat and breathe so much that they told us that she was better enough to go back home and try to do those things there.

How We Got Out of the Hospital

There weren't any other tests or procedures for them to put her through. There wasn't anything else for us to do but for us to go back home and try to keep on living there. The nurse handed me the clipboard so that I would sign the forms to check my wife out of the hospital. My wife could hold onto the pen and move her hand, but she couldn't write her name out right anymore.

I handed the clipboard with the signed forms on it back to the nurse so that we could go back home. I had already packed our two suitcases back up with our clothes and the other things that I had brought to the hospital from our home. I had everything else from the hospital that we needed to go back home too—my wife, her walker, her prescriptions, and the directions for her home care.

One of the hospital workers rolled a wheelchair into her hospital room and helped my wife to sit down in it. He pushed my wife and her wheelchair out of her hospital room, down the hallway, onto and off of the elevator, across the hospital lobby, and out of the hospital.

We got outside of the hospital and I put the walker down in front of my wife so that she could walk with it. She pushed herself up out of the wheelchair and pulled herself forward with the handles of the walker. The hospital worker backed the wheelchair away from my wife and went back inside the hospital. There wasn't going to be anybody else to help us anymore.

My wife walked with the walker and with little steps and I walked beside her with them too. Our lives moved slower then than they ever had before, but we kept going.

We got out to our car and I set our two suitcases down and opened the car door up for her. I stood in front of her and held her up under her arms while she turned around so that she could sit down in the car's front seat. I moved the walker away from her, bent down over her, lifted her legs up under her knees, and slid her legs and her feet into our car with the rest of her body. I pulled the seatbelt out over her shoulder, across her lap, and buckled her in.

I closed her car door and opened the car's trunk. I put our two suitcases and the walker into the trunk and then I got into our car too. I started the engine of our car up, but I was afraid to drive us away from the hospital. I was afraid that she might stop breathing again and that we would need other people to help us keep her alive again. But I was afraid to turn the engine off too. Our car had kept her alive before.

I backed our car out of its parking spot in the hospital parking lot, put it in drive, and drove us back home. I opened her car door, the screen door, and the back door up. I left the engine of our car on until I got her back inside our house. I turned all the lights on inside our house and held all the doors open so that she had enough room to walk through them with her walker.

I would have carried her inside if I could have lifted her up, but I was too old and too tired. We just wanted to go back to bed and back to sleep together so that we could wake up again and it would be morning at home again. But neither one of us could sleep much that night. Our bed seemed to be shaking again. We were both too afraid that one of us might not wake up.

PART TWO

Some of the People I Have Known
Who Have Died

There are a lot of people who I think of lying in a hospital bed, in their bed at home, in their bed at the nursing home, or inside their casket at a funeral home—my Uncle Johnny in a hospital bed with that cut down his chest, my Aunt Anita with her body so bloated in another hospital bed and then so thin in her bed at home, my father no longer able to get up out of his bed at home, my Aunt Billie in the small bedroom downstairs in my grandmother and grandfather's house and then in that single bed in one nursing home and then in another single bed in another nursing home, my Grandfather Kimball inside his casket at that country funeral home, my Grandmother Kimball inside her casket at that same country funeral home, my Grandfather Oliver with his oxygen tank and oxygen mask in that bed in another nursing home, and my Grandmother Oliver in her bed in her bedroom upstairs and then in the bed that they made for her in the living room downstairs after she couldn't really walk anymore and then inside her casket at the front of that long room at the funeral home.

I have visited so many hospitals and nursing homes and funeral homes. I have watched dying people sleep. I have watched them try to talk and try to eat. I have fed them food and read them books. I have gotten them water and given them their pills. I have listened to how hard it was for them to breathe. I have covered them up with blankets and turned their pillows over to the cool side. I have helped them into and out of their beds and into and out of bathrooms. I have gone to get the doctor or the nurse for them.

All of it helped for a little while, but almost all of them died anyway. My Grandmother and Grandfather Oliver both died from something to do with the heart—either failure or disease—and I keep thinking about how she died before he did. She had broken her hip and her ankle, and then there was a pain inside her chest that stayed there and made it hard for her to breathe.

I keep trying to imagine what my grandfather must have been thinking while my grandmother was in and out of the hospital. They both knew that she was going to die soon. They both knew that they had a finite amount of time left with each other after they had been together for so many years. I keep thinking about those last days that they had together, what they must have thought and felt and did, and how those days might have been different from all the other days that they had already lived together.

I keep thinking about how after my grandmother died, that my grandfather started to die too, and that it was so hard for him to breathe in those last few months that he was alive without her. I keep thinking about my wife and how one day one of us is going to die and that the other one of us will still be alive too.

Some of the People Who Came Home from the Hospital

My Uncle Johnny, my Grandmother Kimball, my Grandfather Kimball, and my Grandfather Oliver—they all died inside a hospital. My Grandmother Oliver came home from the hospital for one last time and then died at home a few months after that. My Aunt Anita got out of the hospital and died in her canopy bed a few months after she came home for her last time too. My Aunt Billie got out of the hospital and lived at home for years, even though she never got any better or well. She got worse until none of us could take care of her anymore, and then she lived for so many more years in a nursing home and then another year more in another nursing home before she died in her single bed there.

Nobody ever really got any better. Everybody died inside a hospital or came home from the hospital and died in their bed.

But sometimes there was some kind of hope when people came home from the hospital, that even though they couldn't lift anything up or walk around, that even though they couldn't breathe without an oxygen tank and an oxygen mask or even feed themselves, that they might somehow get better and then stay alive for some long time after that.

We believed that this could happen, but it never did, not for anybody in my family or anybody else that I ever knew. They were all going to get worse in their own bed and among their own things and their own family and somehow dying that way wasn't supposed to be as bad as dying in the hospital in a bed that wasn't theirs.

But the dying always seemed just as bad or worse for them. We could do so much less for them than could be done for them inside a hospital. There didn't seem to be any more comfort in particular sheets or pillows or certain blankets. There didn't seem to be any reassurance in a familiar view through a bedroom window. So their coming home from the hospital must have been for us, the ones of us who weren't dying yet. It must have made us not hurt so much to be able to do the few small things that we could do for them.

But coming home from the hospital also makes me think of my wife after she came home from the hospital after a serious ear surgery. She wasn't going to die, but we wouldn't know if the surgery were successful and if she would hear again until weeks after she had come back home.

There were so many things that could have gone wrong during that recovery period. A little bone inside her ear had been replaced with a tiny metal rod that could have been dislodged if there were any quick movement or any jarring of her head.

The ear surgery also left her equilibrium off. She couldn't sit down or sit up or stand up without me helping her. She could only lie down in bed or on the couch for those first two weeks of her recovery, and then she could sit up a little in a chair after that. She couldn't move or even talk very fast. It hurt her ear for her to move her jaw. She could only eat oatmeal and jello and bananas and toast and she could only drink through a straw. She couldn't talk on the telephone. She could only walk at a shuffle and only with me beside her or behind her and holding onto her and holding her head steady so that it wouldn't begin to spin.

I brought her food and things to drink and I changed her ear dressings for her. I pulled bloody cotton balls out of her ear and then used tweezers to pick off the little strands of cotton that had attached to her ear with dried blood. I dropped antibiotic drops into her ear canal and dabbed an antibiotic salve onto the cut below her ear. I pushed clean cotton balls back into her ear, but only far enough so that the blood wouldn't run out of her ear when she was sitting up.

She slept in our bed by herself and I stayed far enough away so that I would not bother her when she could sleep—even though she still couldn't really hear—but near enough to her so that I could hear her if she woke up or needed anything or needed me.

But we got to where she could take a bath by herself and then I would help her towel dry and get dressed. She wore clothes that she could pull up her legs or button up around her front so that she didn't have to pull anything off over her head. She started to walk back and forth to the bathroom without me holding onto her. There were enough things for her to hold onto along the way there—walls, chairs, doorways, the edge of the bed.

It was weeks later that we were able to sit down at the dinner table again and eat a slow dinner together. She cut her food with a slow knife and moved a slow fork up to her mouth. She opened her mouth and chewed slowly too. But eating that dinner was the first thing that we had done together again in the way that we had always done things together, even if I did have to help her back to bed after we were done.

We knew that she wasn't going to die from her ear surgery and that she was probably going to get her hearing back. She began to hear sounds that had a low pitch—the hum of the refrigerator, the tumble of the dryer, the cycles of the dishwasher, the bass line of a song that she had always liked but never fully heard before.

But we also knew that she was going to die sometime, some years from then, or that I was going to, and that it might be something like all of that—one of us waiting in the waiting room while the other one of us was in the operating room, both of us in the hospital room with one of us waiting for the other one of us to wake up, one of us helping the other one into our car so that we could drive back home, one of us helping the other one sit up or stand up or walk, one of us helping the other one into and out of the bathroom, one of us changing the bandages on the other one and cleaning the blood up with a washcloth, both of us trying to slow that dying down.

PART THREE

Her First Morning Back at Home

We woke up for her first morning back at home and we were both afraid. We looked at each other and looked around the room. We were still old, but neither one of us had died during the night yet. But neither one of us was too sure where we were either. We weren't too used to our bed and our bedroom anymore. There weren't any machines or IVs around our bed. There weren't any doctors or any nurses going into and out of our bedroom. There wasn't anybody else dying in another bed and there wasn't anybody else to help us get up or get out of our bed either.

I got out of our bed and went around to her side of it. She turned the bedcovers back off her legs and turned her legs out so that they were hanging down over the side of the bed. I set her walker down in front of her legs. She pulled and pushed herself up with her arms so that she could stand up. She walked with her walker into the bathroom and I waited for her outside the bathroom door. I listened for the water in the toilet bowl and for the water in the bowl of the bathroom sink.

She opened the bathroom door back up. I carried a chair from our bedroom into the bathroom and set it down in the bathtub. I turned both the hot water and the cold water on until the water got warm enough for us. She tried to lift her arms up so that I could help her lift her nightgown up off her body and over her head. I took my nightclothes off too.

I held onto her arms for her so that she could step over the edge of the bathtub. I waited for her to sit down on the chair before I climbed into the bathtub after her and pulled the shower curtain along the length of the bathtub.

She could make the bar of soap lather up in her hands, but she couldn't wash most of her body with it. She couldn't reach below her knees to her feet or around to her back. Her arms and her hands still felt too heavy for her to hold them up to her head so that she could wash her hair. I lathered the shampoo up in my hands and worked it into her thick gray hair. I rinsed the shampoo out of her hair and off the rest of her body.

I turned the water off and pulled the shower curtain back. I stepped out of the bathtub and held onto her arms so that she could step out of the bathtub too. I held the bath towel out in my arms for her and she stepped out into it. I stepped back and she held her arms out so that I could dry them off for her.

I wrapped the bath towel around her legs and patted them down with it until they were dry too. Her skin was too dry. There was dead skin on her arms and her legs and her back and her face. We had to peel all of it off her so that she wouldn't die any faster than she already was.

I hung her bath towel up on the towel rack and dried myself off with another bath towel. I helped her step into her underwear and pulled them up her legs. I helped her get her arms through her bra straps and hooked her bra together in the back. I helped her push her arms through the sleeves of her housecoat and zipped it all the way up to her neck.

We walked her over to her dressing table so that she could sit down on her chair at her dressing table. She wanted to brush her hair out. She could hold onto the hairbrush for a few brushstrokes, but then her arm would get too tired. Her hair was almost dry by the time that she was done brushing it out.

I walked back into the bathroom and got her walker back out for her. She walked down the hallway and into the kitchen with it and I walked behind her. I pulled a kitchen chair out from the kitchen table for her and she sat down to eat.

Nobody had brought any trays of hospital food into our bedroom, but there wasn't any bread or fruit or milk or anything else fresh in our house either. We were going to have to feed ourselves things that didn't get too old too fast.

I got a box of dry cereal down from the cupboard. I got spoons out of the silverware drawer and cereal bowls down from another cupboard. I filled the bowls up with cereal and I waited for her to start to eat first. I watched her put the spoon in the bowl and then bring the spoon up to her mouth. I watched her chew and swallow the food and then I did it with her too.

I put the cereal bowls and the spoons into the kitchen sink and rinsed some water over them. I sat back down at the kitchen table with her and we looked around the kitchen. We looked at her walker and we looked at each other. We knew that it didn't matter what or how much we ate. We knew that we wouldn't be alive and be together for much longer.

How We Slowed Our Time Down

We found ways to make our days longer. We followed the sun around our house—from our bedroom and the bathroom in the morning, to the kitchen through noon, the living room through the afternoon, and the dining room for the evening.

At night, we turned all the lights in every room of our house on. We turned the lights on the front porch on. We turned the lights on the back porch and over the garage on too. We wanted to keep the darkness that surrounded our house and us as far away from us as we could.

We wanted it to be daytime all the time. We didn't need much sleep anymore anyway. She had saved so much of it up while she was sleeping in the hospital and I wanted to be awake for the rest of the time that she was going to be alive.

We unplugged all the clocks and anything that had a clock on it. We used our extra time awake to slow the rest of our time down. We cooked and ate and sat and talked and waited and moved and walked and we did it all slowed down. There wasn't anything else that we wanted to do but be awake and alive with each other.

How I Rubbed Her Wrinkles Out

I would rub her back and her arms and her legs and her feet. My hands could rub the wrinkles out of her skin and make her feel younger, so that she could stay alive longer. We were trying to stretch the rest of our lives out.

Some of the Things that She Couldn't Do Anymore

We were afraid to close our eyes to go to sleep so we stayed awake for those days that we were back at home. We tried not to look away from each other too much or even blink and we did other things to help us stay awake too. We kept touching each other on the arm or the hair or the face. We kept sitting up or getting up and standing up. We kept setting this egg timer that we had so that it would keep going off and keep us up too.

We ate to stay alive and awake too. We ate all the food inside the cupboards and the pantry and all the food inside the refrigerator and the freezer. We ate everything that we had that was in boxes and jars and bottles and cans and plastic bags. We ate boxes of cereal, cans of fruit and cans of soup, bags of frozen vegetables, and packages of frozen meat. We ate packages of cookies, boxes of crackers, and bags of potato chips.

We boiled water to make coffee and tea and to cook boxes of pasta and bags of rice. We defrosted frozen orange juice and frozen lemonade and drank it from pitchers. We baked layer cakes and loaves of bread with the flour and the sugar that was left in the jars on top of the kitchen counter and with the packages of yeast that made it all rise up.

All of it was food that didn't get too old too fast. But it took us a long time to get up and get to the kitchen to make our food, to sit down and eat our breakfast and our lunch and our supper, to get back up and clean up the pots and pans and the dishes and the silverware and to put everything away again. We moved through our house and our lives so slowly then.

But my wife wasn't getting any better anymore for those days that we were back at home. She began to forget how to live in our house or with me anymore. She forgot what things were or what they were for. We made labels for the refrigerator and the food inside it, for the doors to the kitchen and our bedroom and the bathrooms, for the things that she used in the bathroom, and for the couch and the chairs and the other places where she could sit down. We wrote instructions out for the things that we used around our house—the telephone and the television, the microwave oven and the stove, the toilet and the sinks.

But she still tried to dial the telephone on the touch pad of the microwave oven and put her dirty clothes away inside the dishwasher. Sometimes she sat down on a chair and peed on the cushion and other times she would throw trash away in the clothes hamper.

We moved through the rooms of our house slowly so that I could show her what things were. We turned doorknobs to open doors up and looked into the different rooms of our house to show her what they were for. We turned water faucets on and off. We turned the coffee maker, the lamps, the television, and all the other appliances on and off too.

She was still surprised that turning a switch on made the ceiling fan turn on or made the living room fill up with light. She was still surprised when she heard somebody's voice through the telephone, or when the people on the television started talking or the voices on the radio started talking or singing. She forgot more and more about our house and us until she couldn't always remember my name or why I was helping her get up or eat and then she forgot how to stand up or open her mouth up or say my name or move her arms.

She couldn't get up out of her chair for our walk across the living room to the dining room with her walker. I couldn't help her enough so that she could do it either. So I brought a small table from our spare bedroom out to her in the living room and set it down around her legs. I brought her food out to her too and set it down on the small table in front of her.

It was still too hard for her to sit up and she couldn't lean forward either. Her head had gotten too heavy for her neck and it would fall back against the headrest of her chair and her mouth would fall open a little bit. I would sit down next to her to hold her head up for her so that I could feed her food with a spoon. She couldn't open her mouth very much anymore and she could only chew slowly, but we still had all those long meals together. She would smile as much as she could after she had chewed and swallowed her food.

How Our House
Had Gotten Too Old Too

Our house had gotten too old and started to die too. The paint was peeling off it so that the wood was showing through in places. The wood had gotten soft in places too and there were too many moldy age spots growing on it to replace it.

Some of the shingles had come off the roof and I would find them in the bushes around our house and scattered around the front yard and the backyard too. There were cracks in the windowpanes and the drafty wind that came through them made us feel as if we were back in the cold air of the hospital.

There were also cracks in the ceilings and in the walls. Our house was settling down on its foundation after all those years that we had lived inside it. Our house had started leaking too—through the roof and the ceiling, but also through the basement walls where there were cracks in the foundation. There were water marks on the ceilings and the walls and our house never dried out.

We had roofers and builders and a handyman come out to look at our house, but none of them thought that it should be fixed. They all said that our house was too old and that too much of it needed to be replaced. They didn't say that we shouldn't keep living in it, but they were afraid that part of the roof or the ceiling might fall down on us. They were afraid that our house might flood in a heavy rain and that the foundation might be washed away.

But we couldn't see any sky or anything else except for darkness through any of the cracks in the ceiling and we didn't worry too much about too much rain. We wanted to float away from all of this anyway.

What the Doctor Said that She Needed

My wife moved less and got worse, but she didn't want to go back to the hospital. I got her to go to a doctor, but she couldn't walk enough with her walker to get out to our car and I couldn't lift her up to carry her that far either. She didn't want me to call an ambulance again, so I tried to think of ways to move her.

I thought of things that would roll. I had a wheelbarrow out in the garden and a dolly out in the garage, but she wouldn't have let me help her get in or on either one of those. So I rolled an old desk chair out of our guest bedroom and into the living room. I helped her move from the seat of the living room chair to the seat of the desk chair without her needing to stand up. I raised the seat of the desk chair up so that her feet didn't touch the floor or catch in its wheels. I turned the desk chair on its swivel, held onto the armrests, and pushed her across the living room floor, through the kitchen, and out the back door.

I rolled her down the back walk and around to the passenger side of our car. I helped her slide out of the desk chair and into the seat of the car. I buckled her in, closed her car door, and rolled the desk chair away from our car so that I wouldn't hit it when I backed our car out of the driveway.

The people in the doctor's office brought a wheelchair out to our car so that my wife could get across the parking lot and into the doctor's office. I signed my wife in and we waited in the waiting room. There were other people there who were dying too and we had to wait for them to go first. We waited for them to call my wife's name and then we waited in the examination room.

The nurse helped my wife take all her clothes off. I folded them up and held them in my lap. The nurse helped my wife put a hospital gown on that was cut open down the back and that had little ties on it to hold it together.

The nurse helped my wife get up and lie down on top of the table with the paper stretched over it. It crinkled and ripped when she moved. We talked to the nurse and answered her questions and then we waited for the nurse to come back into the examination room with the doctor.

The doctor told us that she just needed to sleep more. But we told him that we had become afraid of our bedroom and our bed and afraid of sleep. But the doctor told us that she needed to keep taking her pills to keep from having any more seizures and that she needed to take some other pills for sleep.

The doctor told us that she needed to go back to the hospital, but he let us go back to our house. We drove from the doctor's office to the drug store to get her prescriptions filled and get her some other things that we thought might help her.

We bought her pills to reduce pain, to maintain her immune system, to improve her memory, to keep her body tissue from shrinking, and to keep her heart and her lungs healthy enough so that she could feel and breathe. We bought her pills for her joints so that she could move her arms and her hands more and straighten her knees out enough to stand up again. We bought her skin cream to rub the wrinkles out of her skin. We bought her everything else that we could find that might help us keep her alive.

How We Practiced for Her Death

My wife only lived in the living room after we got back home again. I kept thinking that might somehow help keep her alive. We were afraid that if we moved her to anywhere else that she might die, so my wife stayed on the couch in the living room and did the rest of her living there. She slept there and I slept next to her on the floor.

I brought her vitamins and her other pills to take. I put her pills on her tongue and tipped the lip of a glass of water over her bottom lip so that she could swallow them. I fed her food with a spoon and waited for her to chew and swallow. I cleaned the extra food off her lips and her chin with the spoon and then with a napkin after she couldn't eat any more food. I gathered her bottles of pills and the food dishes all up and took them back into the kitchen.

But none of the food that she ate or the pills that she took helped her feel or get any better. We called the doctor up, but he said that he couldn't help her anymore unless we took her back to the hospital. But I couldn't take her back there or think of any other way to help her anymore. She couldn't get up to walk anywhere even with her walker and she couldn't move or talk much anymore either. She didn't want to live as little as she was then, only sitting up or lying down.

So we began to practice for how and when she might finish living and dying. We practiced more seizures, but the shaking made both of us afraid. We practiced strokes, but she was afraid that might leave her only half as much alive as she was then. We practiced heart attacks, but she didn't want her heart to stop first. We practiced overdoses with aspirins and vitamins. We considered slitting her wrists, but we thought that would have hurt too much. We tried to do a suffocation with a pillow, but I couldn't hold the pillow down.

We mostly practiced home death. Neither one of us wanted to go back to the hospital. But we practiced hospital death in case the ambulance came back to our house and took her back there. I got appliances from around our house and plugged them in around my wife—the microwave and the coffee maker, the alarm clock and any other appliances that had lights or numbers that lit up or that made beeps—and then I practiced unplugging them.

It got quiet when we had everything turned off or unplugged. It got hard for her to keep her eyes open anymore either. The breathing sounded hard coming out of her nose and her mouth. So we also practiced for her death with sleep. She would keep her eyes closed and change her breathing and push that hard last breath out of her lungs and her nose and her mouth.

Why We Both Took Her Sleeping Pills

We both took her sleeping pills so that we both could sleep. We were doing everything together that we could.

I kept some of the sleeping pills for myself and put the rest of them in her mouth for her. I lifted the glass of water up to her bottom lip and she lifted her head up off the pillow a little bit. I tipped the water into her mouth and she swallowed all her sleeping pills and started to fill up with sleep.

I swallowed mine so that I could sleep that sleep with her. I didn't want to wake up either. We both held onto each other. We looked at each other before we closed our eyes and let go of her.

Hold onto Me

I could feel you there with me while I slept. Sleeping felt better than being awake. I felt so light without my body around me and holding me down on the couch anymore. I was outside of me and outside of you too, but I didn't rise up or float away.

I watched you wake up and try to wake me up too. I could still feel you touch my face and my cheek. I liked the way you brushed my hair back with your hand. I liked the way you held onto my hands with your hands. They must have felt a little cold and a little wet, but they started to feel warm again when you held onto them. I want you to know that I stayed there with you and held onto you too.

How I Tried to Get Her Back

I could almost hear her talking to me. She was near me or around me, next to me or holding me still. But she was gone too and I hadn't taken enough of her sleeping pills or I wasn't close enough to dying to go with her yet.

But I wanted to get my wife back. I turned the arms on all the clocks in all the rooms of our house back. I rolled the number of the date on my watch back to a day that she was alive on. I got some old calendars out and hung them up on the walls. I called up the old telephone numbers at the places where we used to live. I looked out the back window and into the back-yard until I could see back to years ago. I kept looking behind me, but I couldn't find her standing back there anymore either.

She wasn't living in the living room or getting up off of the couch or out of our bed or taking a shower or fixing breakfast or making lunch or eating dinner or eating out or going out. She wasn't answering the telephone or listening to the answering machine or calling anybody back or sitting in the backyard or breaking a glass or taking her glasses off or the trash out or putting her lipstick on or washing her face or her hands.

She wasn't standing in the doorway or reading a book or looking out the window or at me or at old photographs or listening to old records or turning the radio on and dancing slow dances by herself or looking at herself in the bathroom mirror or brushing her teeth or her hair or touching her make-up up or tucking strands of hair behind her ear. She wasn't picking an outfit out or matching her shoes to her skirt or pulling her shirt on over her head or tucking her blouse down into her waistband or bending down to tie her shoelaces up.

She wasn't rearranging the furniture or preheating the oven or turning the stove on or microwaving anything frozen or waving goodbye or buying a book or a newspaper or a magazine or pumping gasoline or driving our car away down the highway or riding her bike up the driveway or running through the backyard or walking through the living room.

She wasn't looking through the cupboards or locking the windows and the doors or sweeping and mopping the floors or mowing the lawn or doing the laundry or folding the clothes or closing the blinds or shading her eyes or turning the lights off or lighting matches or planting flowers or watering plants or drinking water or mixing drinks or fixing her hair-do up or doing the dishes or stripping our bed down or unbuttoning her shirt or her blouse or unzipping her pants or her skirt or rolling her nylons down her legs.

She wasn't turning the air on or the heat down or falling down and breaking her arm and her hip or getting up or waking up or standing up or sitting down in any armchair or climbing up the front steps or walking up the sidewalk or setting out place settings or sitting down at the dinner table or saying my name or touching my arm or my hair or my face or forgetting my name or my face or looking away or taking her pills or going to the doctor or the hospital or trying to sit up and eat or drink or talk or breathe.

What Part of My Life I Was Living In

I woke up and the television was playing the national anthem and the flag was waving on the television screen. But then the music stopped playing and the flag stopped waving and the station went off the airwaves. The television light blurred my eyes and I filled up with static. I couldn't remember what part of my life I was living in anymore. That we were married was the last thing that I remembered.

PART FOUR

How Much He Cared for Her

My Grandmother Oliver slept on a bed that my Grandfather Oliver had made up for her in their living room. She couldn't get out of bed or get out of the pain that she was in during the last days that she was alive, but she wouldn't let my grandfather call for an ambulance. She wouldn't let him take her to the hospital and she wouldn't go to any more doctors and she didn't want any more of them coming over to their house either.

My grandfather did everything that he could for my grandmother. He tried to make the loss of the use of her body seem less terrible than it must have been for her. He fed her and cleaned her and dressed her and gave her the pills that she was supposed to take. He did anything that she asked him to do, but he was old and sick too. He could only walk and move slowly and sometimes she would get impatient with him. She knew that she wasn't going to be alive for very much longer and she was probably frustrated that she was able to do less and less for herself.

She ate less and sat up less. She couldn't walk on her own and then she couldn't walk with her walker or with her two canes or with any other kind of help that he could give to her. She couldn't stand up and then she couldn't get up, sit up, or even roll over onto her side in the bed. She couldn't change her own clothes or wash or clean her face or anything else. She couldn't feed herself or scratch an itch or rub something that hurt. She couldn't chew solid food and then even swallow soft food.

My grandfather cared for her so much and I keep thinking about what he must have been feeling then. I keep thinking about how he had to learn how to do those things for her and around the house. He had never done the laundry or the dishes or any other kind of cleaning around the house. He had to learn how to cook. He started with soup and with toast and with other food that was easy for him to make and easy for her to eat.

He learned about the laundry—what clothes could be washed together, when to use bleach, and how long things needed to stay inside the dryer—but worried about being away from her when he had to go downstairs to put the laundry in or take it out. He knew that it would take him so long to get back up to her upstairs in the living room, even if he could hear her ringing the metal ringer that he had left for her next to her bed. He wanted to be able to sit there with her so that he would be ready for her when she needed him.

But there wasn't anything that he could do that seemed to make her feel any better or even better enough to want to stay alive. He cared for her so much, but he couldn't make the physical pain leave her body.

They both knew that she wasn't ever going to get up out of that living room bed again. She stopped eating any more food and only drank water and ate ice chips. She stopped taking her pills and died early one morning a few days later, a few hours before she was supposed to wake up.

My grandfather stayed with her for a few hours before he called the doctor and the funeral home. My grandfather knew that was going to be the last time that he was going to be alone with her. But he was also waiting until she had been dead long enough so that she couldn't be revived. My grandmother didn't want to be only that much alive, even though my grandfather wanted her to be alive for as long as she could be.

How Love Can Accumulate
Between Two People

My Grandmother Oliver wrote in her diaries throughout most of her life and they were passed on to me after she died. Other people inherited other things from her. People from her church took her clothes and her shoes. People from her quilting group picked up the boxes of scrap material that were never used, a few unfinished quilts, and packets of needles and spools of thread. My mother got my grandmother's antique sewing machine. My sister got most of her real jewelry and her costume jewelry too.

There were certain holiday dishes that my mother and my sister and my brother's wife each wanted—a series of plates with winter scenes on them, a group of bowls made out of colored glass, some ornate serving dishes that were just used on holidays and birthdays. They split them up with each other, but they all seemed to feel some sense of loss in this. Those holiday dishes meant so much to each of them, maybe the idea or the feeling of a whole family being together, but each one of them only got some of them.

But the diaries were the only things that I wanted from her after she died. I wanted to know what my grandmother had thought about for her whole life. I wanted to know what she wrote about the births of her two daughters and her three grandchildren. I wanted to know what she wrote about her daughter's scarlet fever from when she was little and her daughter's cancer that she died from forty years after that.

I wanted to know what she wrote about her husband's marriage proposal and about their years of marriage that they had together. I wanted to find out what she wrote about her husband's years of heart problems and what she wrote about herself in her last years when her body started to fail and it became difficult for her to walk and to breathe.

But she didn't write down anything about any of these things in her diaries besides that they happened—that my grandfather showed her an engagement ring and that she put it on her finger, that her daughters said their first words and said other cute things as they grew up, that her daughter Anita was sick with fever, that my grandfather went into the hospital for a heart valve operation, that her sister Billie had Alzheimer's disease, that Anita was sick with cancer, that my grandfather was recovering, that he came home and continued to improve, that they went to Billie's funeral, and that they went to Anita's funeral.

There were hair clippings from each of her daughters from when they were babies and then little girls. There is also a little bit of peeled skin from my Aunt Anita, from the last months of her life, that is taped into one of the diary entries. But my grandmother never wrote anything down about being sad or tired or afraid. It was enough to go to the hospital and the doctor's office with them and to take care of each of them when they came back home.

But even all these serious things made up only a small portion of her diary entries for her whole lifetime. Most of the daily entries only noted daily things—if she washed or ironed, who visited the house, who she went out to lunch with, if they ate at home or ate dinner out, the days that she went to the beauty parlor and the kind of hair-do that she got, the clothes and the quilts that she made and who she made them for.

She made and washed and ironed lots of clothes. She ate lunch with lots of different friends and most of her other meals with her family. She visited other cities and countries and hospitals and funeral homes. She knew a lot of people who died of heart attacks and of strokes. It snowed a lot in her life.

I found myself exasperated by her diaries and what I didn't find there. But maybe nobody was ever supposed to read those diaries of hers. Maybe the diaries were just supposed to be for her while she was alive and not for anybody else after she died. But I still wanted to read something about my grandmother's love for my grandfather or about her recognition of his great affection for her.

That was how I started to think about how love can accumulate between two people over and through two lifetimes. And that reminded me of how, whenever I went over to their house to visit them in the evening, they were always sitting down next to each other on the couch in their living room.

The Funeral Home that Had Been Somebody's House

My preoccupation with the dying and the dead started with my Grandfather Kimball when I was fourteen and he was dead. He was the first person who had died in my life and it was the first time that I was going to a funeral. But my mother and my father didn't tell me what to expect when we got out to the funeral home. I only remember that I was told that I had to go, that I had to look nice, and that looking nice meant that I had to comb my hair, wear a belt, and tuck my shirt in.

I got dressed up in my best clothes and the rest of my family did too. We all got into the family car and drove to a little town out in the country where my grandfather had lived. Nobody said anything on the drive out there, but the car windows were open and the driving wind was messing everybody's hair up and making our good clothes seem worn out.

My father parked the family car in a gravel parking lot behind what I thought was somebody's house. I realized later that it had been somebody's house, but that it had become a funeral home. We got out of the family car, walked around to the front of the funeral home, walked up the front steps, opened a screen door, and walked into what must have been somebody's living room and had become the front room of the funeral home.

The screen door closed behind us with a slap against the wood doorframe. The windows in that front room of the funeral home were all open and the wind was blowing through it, but it was still hot and smelled musty inside there.

My mother and my father stopped inside the screen door and my sister and I stopped behind them. My mother and my father were talking to somebody or somebody was talking to them. I don't remember what they said, but I remember that I wasn't included in the conversation and that I started looking around that front room.

I know now that it was the viewing room that we had walked into when we walked into the funeral home, but I didn't know what it was then or why I could see my Grandfather Kimball at the other end of the viewing room all laid out inside his casket.

I knew that he was dead, that his body was going to be inside a casket, that people were going to say nice things about him, and that they were going to bury him in a grave. But I didn't expect it to be so casual—for the funeral home to be somebody's house, for the viewing room to be somebody's living room, and for there to be people standing around talking in somebody's living room while there was a casket with my dead grandfather inside it in the living room too. I thought that I was going to be able to approach my grandfather's casket, and that somehow in that approach that I was going to be able to prepare myself for his death, for him being dead, and for how that was going to feel.

But I wasn't prepared for it. It felt as if I had been punched in the stomach by somebody that I couldn't see when I saw my grandfather's dead body inside a casket and on top of a table in that living room. I didn't know that the casket was going to be open. I didn't know that we were going to have to look at him or that the skin on his face would be so limp that it wouldn't look like his face anymore.

Nobody told me that grief feels like fear. I kept trying to swallow, but my mouth had dried up. My tongue got thick and stuck to the roof of my mouth. My jaw started trembling up and down. I tried to hold my mouth closed with my hand. My eyes started opening and closing too. I tried to keep myself from crying.

I pinched the bridge of my nose. I closed my eyes tight and wiped them dry. I took deep breaths. I don't think that anybody else noticed any of this. My mother and my father stopped talking with those other people. We all walked up to my grandfather's casket.

I remember that my father made me look at his father. I remember thinking that must have been what we were there for. I think that my father thought that was what we were supposed to do too—that we were supposed to look nice, look at the dead body, and then sit down to listen to the nice things that were going to be said about the dead person.

I looked, but then looked away. We all turned away from the casket. We all walked back up to a row of chairs in the front of the viewing room and my father told us to sit down there. They were getting ready to say the nice things about my grandfather.

I'm still surprised about the way I felt when I saw my grandfather's dead body. My Grandfather Kimball wasn't somebody that I had any real affection for. I don't have any nostalgic memories of him. We never played catch or played cards or went fishing. He never pulled any quarters out from behind his ears or had any candy in my pockets. I mostly remember him as somebody to be afraid of, but I don't think that it was my grandfather who made me feel afraid then.

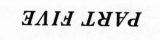

PART FIVE

How They Touched Her As If She Were Still Alive

I put my hand on her chest over her heart, but I couldn't feel anything beating inside her anymore and when I leaned my ear down to her I couldn't hear anything inside of her either. I pulled the blankets down off her body to see if there were anything that I could do for her, but the blood inside her seemed to be draining away from the front of her and down toward her back and into the backs of her legs. It made her face and arms look so pale, but the rest of her turned more purple and more red where the blood started to settle.

Her skin seemed to fall away from her too. It pulled down and showed more of the shape of her face—the flat part of her forehead, the line of her jaw, and the angle of her cheekbones. It showed more of the bones around her collar and her shoulders and down her arms. It seemed to pull her mouth and her eyes open too, but she couldn't see me or talk.

I pushed her mouth back up and pulled her eyelids back down and held them closed until they stayed shut. Her arms were still a little warm, but her hands felt cold. Her skin was a little wet and then it dried out. The rest of her body heat seemed to be leaving her body too, but I tried to keep her warm. I covered her back up with the blankets and I wrapped myself around her on the couch and held onto her too.

She seemed to feel a little warmer again, but that was probably just the body heat from me warming her skin back up. But then she started to feel colder again and heavy in my arms and it made me feel cold too. The hard smells and the gurgling sounds that were coming out of her made me turn my face away. There wasn't anything else that I could do to take any kind of care of her anymore.

I called the funeral home to see if they would come over to my home to take care of my wife for me. I told them that I couldn't keep my wife warm enough anymore. I told them that I couldn't lift her up off the couch and that her legs buckled too much when I tried to help her get up and that she couldn't hold onto me with her arms. They told me that maybe I should wait in another room of our house, but I had to arrange her on the couch before they came over to our house to get her.

I put her arms back down at her sides. I straightened her nightgown out and pulled the blankets back up to her neck. I brushed her hair out with her hairbrush and put her lipstick on her lips. I brushed some powder on her forehead and on her chin and on her nose. I brushed some color onto her cheeks for her.

I heard the van from the funeral home drive up in front of our house and then I heard them turn the engine off so that I couldn't hear it anymore. They walked up the front walk and they knocked on the front door with a soft knock. They came through the front door and into the living room with their metal gurney. They were going to take my wife away from me and our house and with them to their funeral home.

They spoke with soft voices. They called her by her name. One of them pulled her eyelids back up and checked to see if there were anything left inside her eyes, but they couldn't see anything there. He listened for her heart through her chest, but he couldn't hear it either. He took her temperature and some of it was already gone. He cut through the side part of her nightgown so that they could see where the blood had pooled down into the bottom part of her body, but he didn't know why she had died. He said that her heart had probably stopped, but it didn't feel as if it had to me.

They moved her body slowly. They touched her as if she were still alive. They lifted her up and laid her back down on top of the metal gurney. They straightened her arms out and placed them along her sides. They covered her body up and her face up with a clean sheet. They pulled the sheet tight and tucked it in under the metal gurney and around her body so that it held onto the shape of her. They snapped the buttons of the gurney straps and they pulled the straps tight. They tried to do it in a quiet way, but it sounded loud to me.

They rolled the metal gurney and my wife out of our house. They rolled her down the front walk and up to the back of their funeral van. They opened the funeral van's two back doors up and one of them pushed a button that made the metal gurney's legs collapse under her. They lifted her up and rolled the metal gurney and her body into the back of the funeral van. They closed the funeral van's two back doors back up, but I didn't hear the latch click shut even though it must have made a sound.

They both walked back to the front of the funeral van and climbed back up into it. They didn't look back at our house or back at me. They drove away from me with my wife. They didn't turn on a siren or any flashing lights.

The Picture of Her from When She Was Still Alive

The funeral director called me at home and asked me to bring a picture of my wife to the funeral home. He wanted the picture of her to be from when she was still alive and before she got sick. He wanted to see what the color in her skin was and the way her face looked when she smiled.

He asked me to bring some of the clothes that she liked to wear with me too. He said that they could be clothes that she would wear anywhere and every day, but that they were going to have to cut her clothes open in the back so that they could dress her up and lay her out in them.

I picked out a picture of her from when we were on vacation one time. We were next to a lake and the wind was blowing her hair back away from her face so that it showed the way she smiled and her whole face. There was all that water and so much sky behind her that it seemed as if we would always be alive and be together.

I found the red dress that she was wearing in that picture in some boxes of summer clothes that she had put away years ago and never worn again. It hadn't been summer for us for years. I picked out a set of her underwear that matched, a pair of sandals that matched the dress, and a sweater that she could wear over the dress.

I drove the picture of her and her clothes to the funeral home to give them to the funeral director. He thanked me for her things and said that there were some other last things that we needed to talk about. He said that my wife could have a wooden casket or a steel one. He said that the casket could be made out of bronze or copper or stainless steel or a regular steel that came in different kinds of thickness. He said that the casket could be made out of poplar or oak, out of cherry or maple or pine. He said that the casket could be made out of particle board or cardboard. He said that the casket could be made out of ash.

He said that they could cremate her and put her ashes inside an urn or that they could put her body inside a casket and bury her in the ground. He said that they could embalm her so that there could be a viewing of her. He said that they could bury her ashes too or that I could take them home or take them somewhere else and spread them out somewhere she liked, like the lake in the picture of her.

I didn't know how to decide. She had always liked to put her feet in the dirt, but I didn't want her to be buried in the ground so far down away from me. I wouldn't be able to take her home with me. But the weight of the dirt pushing down on her casket didn't seem as bad as her being burned up into little pieces of ash and bone and poured into an urn.

The wood casket sounded more comfortable than the steel one or a ceramic urn, but I picked the steel casket out for her to keep the dirt and the rocks up off her for a longer time. I didn't want all that weight pushing the top or the sides of the casket down or in on her.

I picked out the padding for the casket that was thick and firm but soft. I decided on a lining for the casket that contrasted with the color of her dress, but that was going to match the color of her skin after they put the funeral make-up on her. I picked a pillow out that went with the color of her hair and that was also going to keep her neck from getting stiff.

We had practiced for all this in those last days too. We had used the couch for how she wanted to be laid out inside her casket. She had wanted to get her body position right. She had wanted her hands at her sides and her right side showing out. We had propped her head up on the armrest of the couch so that we could smooth the wrinkles in her neck and her face out for her. She had picked out that red dress that she had wanted to wear from memory and I thought of the sweater that she had always liked to wear at home and that she could wear over the dress and that might help to keep her warm.

How I Had Not Seen Her
Since She Had Died

I had not seen her since she had died and they had carried her out of our house and driven her away from me. But they let me see her again before they showed her to anybody else. They tried to make her look like she had looked. They put make-up on her face and her ears and her neck to replace the skin color that she used to have in those places. They wanted the color of her face inside the casket to match the color of her face in the picture by the lake.

They asked me if they had the color and the style of her hair right. They had fixed her hair up and pulled it back away from her face, but it wasn't the wind or anything natural that made her hair look that way this time. I told them that her hair wasn't the right color anymore, so they colored more of her hair color back on for me with a hair crayon and sprayed more color on it with colored hair spray.

The color of the skin on her neck was already coming off on the collar of her red dress and the sleeves of it cut into the make-up that they had put on her hands up to her wrists. They had drawn more eyebrows above her closed eyes with an eyebrow pencil and thickened her eyelashes up with some kind of mascara that made her look as if she weren't going to open her eyes up again.

They wanted to make a last picture of her for me so that I could think of her when she wasn't sick or dying or dead. But her mouth looked wrong and they couldn't really make her face look like her face looked. Her body wasn't the right body shape anymore either. All of that made her look so different from herself and made her seem so far away from me.

They laid her out inside the casket on a slant. They angled her front shoulder lower than her back shoulder so that she didn't look so flat on her back inside the casket. It made it look as if her body were being lifted up. But they also had her laid down low enough so that the lid of the casket would still close over her without hitting her nose.

They asked me if there were anything that I wanted to put inside the casket with her, but I couldn't think of anything that I wanted her to take with her but me. A picture of me would not have been enough of me and the casket wasn't big enough for both of us to get inside it.

They put her casket and her on top of a table and rolled her out into the viewing room of the funeral home. They said that viewing the person dead was supposed to make it feel as if the person really were dead, but I don't think that it could have felt any more real than it already did. That was my wife inside that casket who was all filled up with embalming fluid and covered up with funeral make-up and dressed up in clothes that didn't look right without her standing up in them.

The make-up and the hair color didn't help. The red dress didn't help and neither did the matching sandals or the sweater that she had liked to wear at home. There were sounds coming out of my mouth and I started to cry even though I didn't think that there was anything else that could have come out of me.

How I Wanted to Get Inside
a Casket Too

Everything inside the viewing room seemed or felt or looked or was dead. The shag carpet smelled musty and damp. The air smelled as if it were filled with exhaled breath. The frame of the chair that I was supposed to sit down on felt as if it were made out of soft and rotting wood.

I got up out of that chair, walked up to her casket, and leaned in over her. I blew a little breath across her made-up and waxy face. Her slack cheek moved in against the wind and then back out. Her lips trembled a little bit and it made my lower lip tremble a little bit too. I held onto my chin to stop my mouth from moving up and down. I breathed deep breaths in until my chest went out and my shoulders went back and I didn't feel as if I were trembling anymore.

I lifted the back collar of her sweater up and tucked the care label in behind her neck. I reached inside her casket and held onto the hand that was closer to me. I held onto her hand with both of my hands. I leaned in to whisper into her ear. I told her that she was still my wife and her earlobe moved a little bit when I said it so that I knew that she could hear me. I placed her hand back inside the casket and at her side and let go of it. I turned away from her casket and moved away from her.

The funeral director came forward and closed the lid of the casket and turned the screws for the lid down. He got a few other funeral workers to help him carry her out of the viewing room and the funeral home and out to the hearse in the parking lot. They slid her casket over those rollers and into the back of the hearse. I wanted to get inside a casket and have them carry me too. I wanted them to slide me into the back of the hearse with her too.

They closed those two back doors to the hearse and we all got into the hearse. They all sat down in the front seat and in the first backseat of the hearse and I sat down in the last backseat that was closest to her.

We drove out of the funeral home parking lot and onto the street. The hearse had those two flags at the front of the hood that made all the other cars out there pull over to the curb so that we could drive past them without slowing down.

We drove through the cemetery gate and into the cemetery along those thin streets that only went one way. We drove out into the back of the cemetery where the new cemetery plots were. The funeral director parked next to a little hill and we all got out of the hearse.

Two of the funeral workers opened the two back doors up sideways so that they could slide my wife and her casket back out of the hearse. They held onto the handles at the foot of her casket and two more of them held onto the handles at the head of her casket as they rolled it out of the hearse.

They all lifted her up onto their shoulders and carried her up the little hill to her grave. They set her casket down on some wide straps that were up over her grave and set her down when they did that. I sat down along one of the long sides of her grave on a graveside chair. The funeral director sat down beside me and the other funeral workers stood behind us. There was a pile of dirt there beside us. They were going to fill my wife's grave in with it after we left.

The funeral director stood back up in front of my wife's casket. He looked up over all of us and up into the sky. He said a few words that I couldn't really hear or couldn't understand. There was some kind of roaring sound inside my ears that kept me from hearing anything outside of me. The funeral director looked at me and then looked away and down. I looked down and away from them too. I kept looking at the empty chair sitting next to me and kept thinking about my wife sitting down on it.

I think that the funeral director said something to me and that I was supposed to say something or do something. I opened my mouth, but I couldn't get any words to come out of it or move my hands to say anything either.

The funeral director looked back up at me and I think that I nodded at him and that he motioned two of the other funeral workers over to her grave where there were these two cranks. They each released a crank to lower my wife and her casket down into her grave. They stopped when her casket hit the bottom of the grave and made a noise and then they let the cranks go down a little bit more.

I think that the funeral director asked me if I wanted to throw the first handful of dirt into her grave, but I couldn't get myself to bend down or pick up any dirt to throw it on her casket. I couldn't help to cover her up unless it was with a blanket and only if her face were still showing. So one of the other men threw the first handful of dirt into her grave and it made a dusty, splattering noise on top of her casket.

They all waited for me to stand up and walk away from her grave and then they followed me back to the hearse. I could see a little ways off that there were two other men standing there with shovels. They were waiting for us to leave so that they could fill her grave in with that pile of dirt.

We all got back into the hearse and drove out of and away from the cemetery. It was the first time that I was going to be away from my wife for such a long time.

Thank You for Looking at Me
for So Long

Thank you for giving them the sweater for me to wear and for tucking the care label in for me. I didn't want you to stop looking at me or holding onto my hand. I didn't want them to close the casket.

They were so gentle with me when they carried me and lowered me down into the grave. The dirt and the rocks sounded like a heavy rain falling down on top of the casket that would not let up. Then it sounded muffled and then hush and then it got quiet. But I could hear you driving away and I could hear you thinking about me. I wanted you to hear me back so that you didn't miss me so much or for so long.

PART SIX

The Viewing Room of the Funeral Home

There were three days of viewing at the funeral home before my Grandmother Oliver's funeral and her burial. My Grandfather Oliver and the rest of the people in our family who were still alive stayed in the viewing room of the funeral home for all the viewing hours on all those viewing days. My grandfather sat up near the casket on a chair with a long back and one of the rest of us—my mother, my brother, my sister, his sister, or me—always sat with him.

The people who my grandmother and my grandfather had known, all of them who weren't already dead, they would walk into the viewing room, walk up to my grandmother's casket, and look at her face and her hair and her hands. They would maybe touch the side of her casket, maybe say a prayer, and then turn away from her casket to walk over to my grandfather to say something to him.

They would usually say something about what a wonderful or a generous or a kind and loving woman that my grandmother was and how lucky we all were to have known her for the time that we did. Any of this was true. She was. We were. But they would also usually say something about need, how if my grandfather needed anything, if there were anything that they could do for him, that he should let them know. But there wasn't anything that he needed then except for his wife to be alive and back at home with him.

I keep thinking about each of us sitting in the viewing room with my grandfather and how that must have been our family's attempt to approximate my grandmother and how she sat with my grandfather for all the years that they were married—how they sat together at the kitchen table, the dining room table, and on the couch in front of the television in their living room.

I keep thinking about how I watched all those people go up to my grandmother inside her casket to give her their last respects. I had given mine, but I couldn't look at her inside that casket for very long.

There wasn't anything there that reminded me of my grandmother and how she was when she was alive, except for the dress with the flower print on it that she had made for herself and that they had dressed her body up with.

Everything else seemed wrong—the unnatural color that her hair had become after she died, how her face and her neck and her hands were thick with that funeral make-up, the strange way that they had made her hair up so much curlier than it had ever been when she was alive, and even that she was even dead and laid out inside that casket inside a viewing room with all those other people looking at her. I didn't want to remember any of it.

This is why I am still surprised when I think about my grandfather taking pictures of my grandmother inside her casket inside that viewing room. My grandfather had gotten up out of his chair with the long back, walked up to the casket that held his wife inside it, and held his instant camera up to his face. He looked through the viewfinder of his instant camera for a long time before he took any pictures of her and I keep thinking about how the camera lens was turning her upside down and then right side up again and that that might have somehow made her look and seem alive again through some trick of mirrors or perspective or light.

Or maybe it was the way that a picture of her brightened in his hands after it came out of his instant camera, the way that she turned from some kind of filmy gray back into all of the colors that she had been. My grandfather held her in his hands. He blew on each fresh picture of her and waved it back and forth and waited for her to materialize before him.

How His Heart Hurt

My Grandfather Oliver said that his heart hurt. We thought that it was my grandmother who he was talking about and it probably was, but it was also that his physical heart, the muscle in his chest, hurt. Breathing had become difficult for him after she died. It was probably difficult for him before she died too, but none of us had noticed it then, and he hadn't said anything about it or about any pain in his chest. I'm not sure that he had noticed it before either. We were all so focused on my grandmother back then. We could only pay attention to one dying person at a time.

My grandfather went to the doctor and the doctor told him that his heart valves were clogged and weak, that there wasn't enough blood being pumped out of his heart and through the rest of his body, that he needed to have a heart valve operation, but that he wasn't strong enough to have the operation then. The doctor gave him an oxygen tank to help make breathing easier for him, to keep him alive, and to maybe help him get his body and his heart strong enough again so that he wouldn't die if they could perform the heart valve operation on him.

My grandfather's heart had become weak. He had given everything in it away to my grandmother as she was dying. The lack of blood pumping into and out of his heart also meant that he would sometimes black out. His brain would stop when there wasn't enough blood flowing through it and he would be dead for a little bit.

He said that he would wake up again and try to remember where he was and what year it was. He said that his chest would hurt and that his head felt as if somebody were squeezing it and that he would try to remember where my grandmother was. I'm still not sure if my grandfather separated the physical and the emotional pain.

It was because of this that my mother hired a woman to help my grandfather out at home. The woman was supposed to come to his house for a few hours of each day. She was supposed to clean the house up, do the laundry, do the dishes, and do any other household chores that she could. She was supposed to make lunch and then make a dinner that my grandfather could warm up to eat later that night.

But my grandfather said that the woman didn't clean right, that the food that she cooked tasted wrong, and that he wouldn't let her come back to his house. He didn't say that she didn't do any of these things the way that my grandmother would have done them, but that was probably what he meant.

I think that it made my grandfather's heart hurt more, that other woman doing those daily things in the house that he had shared with my grandmother for all those days and for all those years. My mother tried to hire another woman to help out, but my grandfather wouldn't even let her come into the house. The woman said that he wouldn't get up to come to the front door. She said that at first she thought that he was hurt, but that when she cupped her hands around the sides of her eyes and looked hard through the window that he was just sitting there in his chair looking at what looked like an old picture album. My grandfather was hurt, but none of us could get inside of him—not the doctor, not the pictures, not his sister or daughter or any of his grandchildren—to make it stop.

My grandfather couldn't keep himself enough alive then. He needed the oxygen tanks filled up and changed. He needed the food that other people made. My mother tried to help him when he would let her. She worked fulltime and also had her own house to keep up, but she would go over to his house every night after work after my grandmother had died. She would pick up a few things, make sure that my grandfather had something to eat, make more food for him to warm up, and make sure that there was enough oxygen for him inside his oxygen tank. My grandfather didn't want my mother doing these things for him either, but she had keys to his house and could let herself in.

This wasn't just that my grandfather didn't want other people doing these things for him. I think that he knew that he was going to die soon too. He didn't think that he needed to keep the house clean anymore. He didn't think that he was going to be alive long enough for it to get too dirty. He didn't think that he needed to do the dishes anymore either. My grandmother and he had accumulated so many glasses and bowls and plates and so much silverware over the years that they had been married that he thought that it would be weeks before he didn't have something clean to eat with or on.

My grandfather also wouldn't buy any new clothes for himself. He put cardboard inside his shoes to cover up the holes in the soles of them and he wore two pairs of socks so that the holes in his socks didn't show through either. There were places in the shoulders and the elbows of his dress shirts that had worn so thin that you could see his skin through the weave of the cloth. The shirt cuffs and the shirt collars were frayed. The cuffs of his suit jackets were frayed too and some of the pockets were missing or torn.

He sewed patches on the elbows on his suit jackets and on the knees of his suit pants. There were holes in them from when he had blacked out and fallen down. But my grandfather wouldn't wear any of the new clothes that we bought for him. He left them inside their shopping bags with the price tags on them. Somebody returned them to the store after he died.

How He Tried to Communicate
with Spirits

My Grandfather Oliver believed that living people can communicate with the spirits of people who are dead. He believed that he had witnessed this when he was a child and lived with his Uncle L.P. who was a spiritualist medium.

He said that his Uncle L.P. could do what was called a corner séance. His Uncle L.P. would sit in the corner of a room that had all its curtains pulled closed so that no outside light could get into it. An oil lamp would be placed on the floor in the middle of the room, though the light from it had to be kept low and shaded so that Uncle L.P. didn't go blind or die.

Uncle L.P. would play a trumpet until his eyes rolled back inside his head. He would stop playing and start to shake. The voices of other people would start to come out of his mouth or the spirits would start to form out of the light from the oil lamp and speak through their own mouths.

The spirits and the voices would say how and when and where they died. They would answer any of these questions about any other dead people and they would take messages or questions back to the spirits of other dead people.

My grandfather said that when his Uncle L.P. would begin to get tired, the voices of the spirits would start to get quiet or their forms would start to dissolve into a weak fog that seemed to slip away down into the floorboards. Uncle L.P. would collapse down into his chair in the corner of the room and his eyes would roll back out of his head. Somebody would put the oil lamp out and Uncle L.P. would stand up. They would open the curtains back up and somebody would bring a glass of buttermilk and a plate of warm biscuits with honey on them into the room so that Uncle L.P. could eat and drink to get his strength and his voice back.

It doesn't matter to me if this were truth or fiction. It only matters to me that it seemed true to my grandfather. He believed it and it was a comfort to him. It helped him to make sense of the death of his mother and of his father, the death of his daughter, and then the death of his wife. He believed that he could talk to all of them after they had died.

This is part of the reason that my grandfather learned how to communicate with the dead too. He would write questions down on little slips of paper and the spirits would answer him in the form of knocks on the walls or on the wood furniture. One knock meant no. Two knocks meant they didn't know. Three knocks meant yes.

My grandfather told my grandmother about the code of knocks and asked her to come back to him to talk to him if she died before he did. My grandfather said that there was a lot of knocking on their bedroom furniture after my grandmother died, but that he never could understand all of it. He believed that the knocking was her, that her presence was meant to be reassuring, and that she was telling him that there was another world after the one that he was living in then.

But the house that my grandmother and grandfather lived in was old too. It made lots of sounds at night—the foundation settling down, the wind in the chimney, maybe footsteps on the floorboards, maybe a knocking sound in the walls.

How I Hear Voices

I tried to communicate with my Grandfather Oliver after he died. I wrote questions down on little slips of paper and kept them in my pockets waiting for answers for them. Sometimes, I still find the little slips of paper in the pockets of jackets that I haven't worn since it was last cold.

I lay awake at night and thought of questions to ask my grandfather. I listened for the knocks on the bedroom furniture or for the footsteps on the old wood floors of the house that I live in with my wife, but I never heard anything that might be an answer from him. Still, sometimes I think that what I may be doing is channeling voices. I hear people who aren't here saying things to me and I write them down.

PART SEVEN

How I Couldn't Take Any of My Funeral Clothes Off

I went back inside through the back door and walked back to what used to be our bedroom. I was going to take my funeral clothes off, but it felt too difficult to untie my tie or my shoes. It felt too difficult to unbutton my shirt or my pants. I couldn't take my suit jacket off. It fit a little tight around my shoulders and it felt as if my wife had her arms around me.

My funeral clothes were all that were holding me together then. I was afraid that I would start to forget my wife if I took any of them off. But I didn't know what else to do after her funeral was over and my wife was buried inside a casket under the ground and I was back inside our house. I kept waiting for her to come back home to me or back to life.

I walked back down the hallway, into the living room, and sat down in a chair. I got up out of the chair and then I sat back down in it. I looked out the window, out into the backyard, and then looked back inside myself.

I didn't want to look inside me or be inside myself anymore, but I kept thinking of things that I wanted to tell her—that I liked the dress that she was wearing, that I didn't know what I was supposed to be doing, that I was going to bring her some flowers and her hairbrush and a change of her clothes when I came to see her soon.

I kept thinking of her grave and her inside her casket and all the dirt on top of her and between us. I wanted to dig her casket up and stand it up and open it up. I wanted her to be standing up and for her to step out of her casket and step back into our living room with me.

I always liked the way that she stood in a doorway and the way that she walked into any room. I always liked the way that she chewed her food and the way that she drank from a glass and I wondered if she could feel hungry or thirsty.

I didn't think that there could be any insects inside her casket yet and I wondered if she itched and I thought of the way that her nose wrinkled up when she didn't like something. I wondered if the insects would mess her hair up or get under her clothes and bite her skin like they always did.

I always liked the way that she took her clothes off and put her clothes on. I always liked the way that she said my name and touched my hair. I kept waiting for her to come back home and touch my hair and say my name.

How I Danced with the Floor Lamp

I pulled one of my wife's dresses off a hanger in her closet and pulled it down over the length of a floor lamp. I pulled a hat of hers down over the lampshade. I glued a pair of her shoes down onto the base of the floor lamp and waited for the glue to dry. I plugged the floor lamp into an outlet in the living room, turned the floor lamp on, and her head lit up.

The dress was full length and it had long sleeves. I held onto the cuff one long sleeve of her dress with my palm and fingers and tucked the cuff of the other long sleeve into my waistband at the small of my back. I placed my other hand behind the long stand of the floor lamp just above where the base of her spine would have been if the floor lamp were my wife.

I waited for the music to start playing inside my head. I pulled the floor lamp up against my body and felt the heat from the light on my face. I tipped the floor lamp back with my one arm and leaned over with her. I stood back up and spun the floor lamp away from me along the edge of its round base and along the length of my arm and the long sleeve of her dress. The base of the floor lamp made a scraping noise against the hardwood floor and so did my shoes.

I could see myself dancing with her on the living room walls. I could see the shadows of us dancing on the walls all the way around the living room.

How I Lay Down in the Cemetery
Grass with Her

I stood in the bathroom over the bathroom sink and stared at myself in the bathroom mirror. I leaned my face in close to the bathroom mirror so that I could only see parts of my face—one eye and then the other eye, each side of my nose, parts of both ears, the wrinkles around my eyes and my mouth. I was trying to see my wife inside my eyes, but I couldn't see her anywhere on my face anymore, so I needed to go see her.

I was going to take her some of her things. I pulled some of her other dresses off their hangers in her closet and laid them out on our bed. I took some of her blouses and skirts off their hangers and laid them out in matching outfits. I picked out matching shoes and matching boots.

I pulled a few days of clean underwear out of one of her dresser drawers—matching sets of her underwear, pairs of nylons and pantyhose and tights and socks. I picked a few of her nightgowns out of another one of her dresser drawers and a housecoat out of her closet. I got a spring jacket and a winter coat out of the coat closet and a hat and gloves that matched them both.

I folded her clothes up and stacked them up in little piles on our bed. I got her suitcase out, laid it out on top of our bed, and packed up all those clothes inside it. I opened her jewelry box up and untangled some of her necklaces and paired up some of her earrings. I went back into the bathroom for her hairbrush, her box of curlers, her make-up kit, and some of her other things from the bathroom. I put all those things inside the suitcase and closed the suitcase up and snapped its locks closed.

I carried her suitcase out of our bedroom, down the hallway, out the back door, and out to our car in the driveway. I set her suitcase down, opened the trunk up, and laid her suitcase down flat in the bottom of the trunk. I went back into the backyard to the tool shed and got a shovel and a rake out too. I dug up some of the flowers from the backyard and then filled the flower hole in the backyard back in. I carried the flowers and the shovel and the rake back out to our car and put them in the trunk too.

I got into our car and turned the engine on. I looked into my sideview mirror and watched the exhaust come out of the tailpipe. It was gray and soft and seemed to slip away up into the air before I expected it to be gone.

I backed our car out of the driveway, put our car in drive, and drove the way to the cemetery where my wife's grave was and where my wife was too. I parked next to the little hill, got out of our car, and opened the trunk up. I got the shovel and the rake out and carried them up the little hill to my wife's grave. I walked back down to our car to get her suitcase and to carry it back up the little hill to my wife's grave too.

There wasn't any grass covering her grave up yet, but there was that thick blanket of dirt. I picked the shovel up and dug enough of the dirt up to bury her suitcase in her grave with her casket and her. I dug some more dirt up next to the headstone and planted the flowers there. I filled those holes back in with the shovel and the dirt and then raked the dirt smooth again.

I lay down in the cemetery grass next to my wife's grave and thought of us lying next to each other in our bed again. I rolled over onto my side and laid my arm out over the dirt and tried to hold onto my wife again.

How I Was Afraid to Wash
the Smell of Her Off Her Clothes

I pulled some dirty clothes out of the laundry basket and found some of her dirty clothes buried down at the bottom of it. They were some of the last clothes that she had worn when she was still alive. I pulled them up out of the laundry basket and separated her clothes from my clothes. I was going to wash her clothes in a separate load.

But I held the ball of her clothes up to my face and smelled them and that made me afraid to wash the smell of her off them. I folded her clothes up and stacked them up into a little pile. I got a plastic bag out and set that little pile of her clothes down inside it.

I tied the ties up on the plastic bag tight. I wanted to keep as much of the smell of my wife on those clothes and with me for as long as I could.

Thank You for the Suitcase of Clothes

Thank you for coming to see me and lie down with me. Thank you for putting your arm around me. I could feel the weight of your body next to me. I could feel the warmth of your body next to me.

Thank you for bringing me the flowers. Thank you for bringing me the suitcase with the changes of clothes and the make-up and the jewelry inside it. I had wanted to get that funeral make-up off my face and my neck and my hands for days. I had wanted to change out of my funeral clothes and I want you to change out of yours soon too. Most of mine were cut open down the back and I could just pull them off, but I had to scrape the funeral make-up off with my fingers and my fingernails.

I didn't want to wear those clothes or look like that or stay there forever. I wanted to travel with that suitcase back home to you so that I could be with you again. I wanted to come back home to get you so that we could go away to somewhere else together. I wanted to go back to sleep with you again. I wanted you to stay and sleep with me.

The Little Pieces of Her that Were Still Her

I kept walking through the rooms of what used to be our house and kept looking for her there. Her absence was everywhere, but there were also little pieces of her everywhere that I looked. There were pictures of her up in frames on the walls and there were pictures of her laid out in albums. There was an armchair that she used to sit in that had a depressed seat cushion and that made me see her sitting there in that armchair.

She left the shape of her sleeping body in the sheets on her side of our bed. The mattress was old and soft too and there were deep places where her shoulders and her back and the backs of her legs had rested.

There was a deep hollow where the back of her head had been and there was also the smell of her hair on the pillowcase.

I found her toenail clippings at the foot of our bed. I found an unwashed glass in the kitchen sink that had her lip print around the rim.

I thought that I saw her thick gray hair in the dark of the broom closet, but it was just a mop that was standing up inside there. I found strands of her hair in the drain catch of the bathroom sink and I wished that I had kept her hairbrush with me for the hair of hers that must have been caught up in its bristles.

I looked out the living room window and saw her out in the backyard. I went to the back door and opened it up, but I couldn't see her out there anymore.

How I Got Ready to Go Away with Her to Sleep

I woke up and my wife was back at home with me. She was standing at the end of our bed and she sat down on the edge of it after I woke up and sat up. She was wearing one of the nightgowns that I had packed up for her inside the suitcase that I had buried with her.

She looked thinner and cold. I told her that I would bring her more food in the morning and I tried to get her to get under the bedcovers with me, but she disappeared when I tried to put my arms around her to keep her warm.

There was dirt on her nightgown and in her hair. There was dirt under her fingernails and covering her arms. I tried to brush the dirt off her arms, but it stuck to her skin.

I got up and got another nightgown out of her dresser drawers for her, but she had brought her suitcase back home with her. She opened it up and got another change of clothes out of it—a clean dress and a warm sweater, some clean underwear and pantyhose and a pair of shoes that matched. She got her winter coat out and her winter gloves and her winter hat too.

She got dressed back up and she looked warm again. She said that she wanted to come back home so that she could go back to sleep with me. She told me that I should go back to sleep too.

I changed out of my nightclothes and put some warmer clothes on too. I put clean underwear and a clean undershirt on. I put a dress shirt, a nice tie, and a clean suit on. I tied the tie up in its knot. I pulled dress socks on and put dress shoes on too.

I got a suitcase out and packed one up for me too. I packed up socks and underwear. I packed up undershirts and dress shirts and shirts for every day. I packed up another suit inside the suitcase and another pair of shoes. I packed up my slippers and my other nightclothes.

I packed up so many changes of clothes and set my suitcase down next to her suitcase. I put my overcoat on over my clothes and put a hat on to keep my head warm. I was ready to go away with her to sleep.

Michael Kimball is the author of three critically-acclaimed novels, including *Dear Everybody* and *The Way the Family Got Away*. Each of his novels has been translated (or is being translated) into many languages. His work has been featured on NPR's *All Things Considered* and in *Vice*, as well as *The Guardian*, *Prairie Schooner*, *Post Road*, *Open City*, *Unsaid*, and *New York Tyrant*. He is also responsible for *Michael Kimball Writes Your Life Story* (on a postcard), the documentary films *I Will Smash You* and *60 Writers/60 Places*, and the conceptual pseudonym, Andy Devine.